A KILLER ENDING

A SNUG HARBOR MYSTERY

KAREN MACINERNEY

GRAY WHALE PRESS

For Lee Strauss, author extraordinaire, with gratitude.

Without that long September beach walk in Florida (and your intriguing and wise suggestions), Snug Harbor, Maine—and Max Sayers—would not exist.

Thank you from all three of us!

_T_wo years ago, if you'd told me I'd be spending the day after my 42nd birthday driving north on I-95 with all of my worldly possessions hitched to my Honda CRV in a U-Haul trailer like some sort of oversize snail shell, I'd have told you you were crazy.

But things change.

Boy, do they change.

It wasn't the best time to head out of Boston. It had been after two o'clock on Friday afternoon when I had gotten the last picture of my two darling girls packed up into a box and loaded into the back of the trailer. Since it was the first weekend of summer vacation in Massachusetts, I was now trapped on the highway with several thousand fellow motorists, many of them with kayaks or bicycles strapped to the backs of their SUVs. Like a lot of them, I was headed north to the Maine coast to enjoy a sunny, sparkling summer weekend. Unlike them, however, I didn't plan to come back on Sunday.

Or at all.

Just three months earlier, listening to a deep gut instinct

for the first time in almost two decades, I'd signed a stack of paperwork, plunked down my life savings, and purchased my very own bookstore, Seaside Cottage Books in Snug Harbor, Maine. With the help of an assistant, I'd spent the last several weeks clearing out years of debris from the storage room, dusting the shelves, taking stock of the inventory, and using what little money I had left to add a carefully curated selection of new books. I'd also spent a good bit of time redecorating the place, rolling up my sleeves and repainting the walls a gorgeous blue, making new, nautical-print cushions for the window seats with my mother's old sewing machine, and scouring second-hand stores for the perfect cozy armchairs to tuck away in corners.

The grand re-opening celebration was scheduled for tomorrow night, and I was as nervous as... well, as nervous as a middle-aged, recently divorced woman who's just spent everything she has on a risky venture in a small Maine town can be. I'd used my final pennies (and a small loan) to take out ads in the local paper and spread flyers all over town; I hoped my marketing efforts worked.

From his crate behind me, Winston, my faithful Bichon-mystery-mix rescue, whined. I reached back to put my fingers through the grate and pat his wooly white head; he licked my fingers. "I know, buddy. But once we get there, you'll get to go for walks on the beach and sniff all kinds of things. I promise you'll love it." He let out a whimper, but settled down.

Walks on the beach. Fresh sea air. A business that allowed me to be my own boss. A home to call my own. I repeated these sentences like a mantra, as if they could wipe the memory of the complicated and painful last year-and-a-half from my mind and my soul.

Move forward, Max. Just move forward.

I took a deep breath and let my foot off the brake unconsciously. The car rolled forward and I slammed on the brake again, just in time to avoid rear-ending the Highlander in front of me, which had four bikes strapped to the back. Two adult bikes, and two smaller pink and blue sparkly bikes, one of which had pink ribbons trailing from the handlebar grips. Two daughters. My eye was drawn to the heads in the car: a happy family, going to Maine for the summer. A dull pain sprouted in my chest, but once again, I banished it.

Forward, Max.

By the time I reached the exit for Snug Harbor, the sun was low in the sky and my stomach was growling. I glanced back at Winston, who was still giving me a reproachful look from his dark brown eyes.

"We're almost there," I promised him.

I turned at the exit. Within moments, we'd left the impersonal, clogged highway behind and were heading down a winding rural route, passing handmade signs offering firewood for sale, a sea glass souvenir shop, and a log-cabin-style restaurant advertising early-bird lobster dinners and senior specials. I hooked a left at a T-intersection marked by a large planter filled with dahlias and white salvia. And then, as if I had crossed the threshold into another world, I was in Snug Harbor.

I glanced at Winston; he was perking up as I tooled down Main Street, which was already buzzing with summer visitors, and when I opened the windows and let the cool, fresh sea breeze in, he sat up and started sniffing. Quaint, homegrown shops faced the narrow, car-lined street, which was landscaped with trees and flower-filled planters. Business appeared to be booming; a line snaked out the door of Scoops Ice Cream, Judy's Fudge Emporium was hopping, and lots of relaxed-looking families strolled the streets with ice cream cones and dreamy smiles. Live guitar music drifted out of the Salty Dog Pub as we rolled by, and I caught a whiff of fried clams that made my mouth water. I'd have to splurge on dinner out soon, I told myself. I just hoped a lot of those vacationers were looking for good reads to relax with on their hotel and rental-house porches so I could support my deep-fried seafood habit.

As I crested the gentle hill, passing the town green on my left, the street in front of me seemed to fall away, leaving a perfectly framed view of Snug Harbor.

The water was a beautiful, deep blue, and beyond it nestled the pristine, tree-clad Snug Island; the tide was low, so the sandbar connecting Snug Harbor to the small island across the water was visible. As I rolled down the street, the whale-watching boat came into view; the big white vessel was just pulling out for its sunset tour. Beyond it, I could see the four masts of the *Abigail Todd* as it sailed out of the harbor toward the small, outlying islands.

It took my breath away, just as it had the first time I'd seen it more than thirty years ago, when I'd spent summers here at my parents' camp on a nearby lake.

I drove down to the end of main street and the pier, which was filled with a mix of working boats and pleasure boats (including a few large yachts), then turned left on Cottage Street.

I passed three dockside restaurants featuring lobster boils and fisherman's dinners, catching yet more whiffs of fried clams (this was going to be an occupational hazard), the cobalt harbor peeking out between the buildings and snow-white seagulls calling and whirling overhead in the evening light. There was a little blue-painted shop called Ivy's Seaglass and Crafts, which I knew housed an eclectic assortment of local jewelry and artwork, and then, on its own, a little way down the street, the walkway flanked by pink rosebushes... Seaside Cottage Books.

My new home... in fact, my new life.

I looked at the familiar Cape-style building with fresh eyes, admiring the gray-shingled sides of the little house, the white curtains in the upper windows, the pots of red geraniums looking fresh and sprightly in half-barrels on the newly painted porch. Two rockers with handmade cushions awaited readers. Behind it, I knew, a beach-rose-lined walkway led down to a rocky beach; a beach Winston and I would be able to walk every morning, greeting the sun. And the bookstore itself—it was a dream come true for me. A place where I could connect with other people who loved books, and introduce others to literary treasures that would open up their minds and their worlds.

Pride surged in me at the sight of the book display that graced one of the sparkling front windows—a hand-selected variety of Maine-centric books and beloved reads, including several of Lea Wait's delightful Maine mysteries, two books by Sarah Orne Jewett, a whimsical book by two young women who had hiked the Appalachian Trail barefoot, and —a personal favorite for years—Bill Bryson's *A Walk in the Woods*. They were like old friends welcoming me home, even though I'd just left my home of twenty years for the last time this morning. I smiled, feeling a surge of hope for the first time that day. A sign with the words OPEN SOON was hooked on the door, and I found myself envisioning the community of readers who would gather here.

Goose bumps rose on my arms as I pulled into the gravel drive beside the small building, carefully easing in the trailer behind me so as not to knock over the mailbox. I parked next to the rear of the house, so that it would be a short trip from the trailer to the back door of the shop. And the back door of my home, which was an apartment on the second floor with a cozy bedroom, a small kitchen and living area, a view of the harbor, and even a balcony on which I planned to put a rocking chair and enjoy my morning coffee, as soon as I could afford it.

My store.

My home.

It was the first time in my whole life I'd had something that was completely and totally mine, and I told myself in that moment that I'd do anything to keep anyone else from taking it away from me.

Of course, at the time, I had no idea someone would try quite so soon.

Like tomorrow.

~

"HEY, MAX!"

As I clambered out of the Honda, a bright-faced young woman opened the back door of the shop and stepped out to meet me.

"What are you still doing here?" I asked.

"Just finishing up a few last minute things for the big opening tomorrow," she said. "My mom lent us some platters for cookies, I borrowed two coffee percolators from Sea Beans, and I've got a line on a punch bowl, too."

"You're amazing," I said, smiling. Bethany had been my right-hand woman in getting the bookstore up and running. She'd been crushed when the previous owner, Loretta Satterthwaite, became too ill to carry on with the store, and had banged on the front door two days after I bought the shop. I'd greeted her with cobwebs in my hair—I'd been dusting—and she talked me into an "internship."

"Snug Harbor needs a bookstore," she'd said. "Plus, I plan to be a writer, so I need to keep up with happenings in the industry."

"What about the library?"

"Their budget for new books is meager. I've volunteered there for years," she told me, "but Snug Harbor without a Seaside Books... it's like having a body without a heart." Since I felt much the same way—I'd spent many summer days holed up in the shop as a girl—I felt an immediate kinship. She smiled, and I noticed the freckles dotting her nose and the bright optimism in her fresh-scrubbed, young face. She reminded me of my daughters, Audrey and Caroline, and my heart melted a little bit. "I'll start as an intern; once the store opens, we'll figure something out. I live with my parents and I'm only taking classes part-time. I've got both ample time and a scholarship."

"I can't pay you much," I warned her. "I'm not opening for months and I spent almost everything on the building."

"I'm sure we'll come to a suitable arrangement," she'd announced, peering past me at a jumble of books Loretta had left on a table. "I'll start by rescuing those poor books from their current condition," she'd informed me, and walked right into the store—and into my life.

Thank heavens for angels like Bethany.

Now, as I stood outside Seaside Cottage Books the day before the grand opening, the sight of a cheerful Bethany in jeans and a pink flannel shirt lifted my heart.

"How's it going in there?" I asked.

"Everything's ship-shape," she announced. "I've got the Maine section finished up—two local authors dropped their books by today—and I picked up more coffee and creamer, and some hot chocolate for the little ones."

"Terrific," I said, feeling better already. "Give me the receipts, and I'll reimburse you!" I opened the back door of the SUV and picked up Winston's crate, setting it on the ground. "There is one thing, though," Bethany said.

"Oh?"

"A rather insistent woman has stopped by three times today," she informed me as I liberated Winston from his crate.

"Who?" I asked as my fluffy little dog shook himself all over and trotted over to greet Bethany. He'd been my faithful companion since I'd retrieved him from the pound six years ago, covered in mange and painful-looking sores and looking a little like a scabby goat. With lots of TLC and medication, we'd taken care of the mange and sores, along with the worms and other maladies that had kept him curled up on the couch with me the first few months. Now, he was bouncy, curious, and suffering from a bit of a Napoleon complex, particularly (alas) with dogs that were more than ten times his size. He'd doubled in bulk since I adopted him, and was a terrible food scavenger. To my delight, since the first day at the pound when he climbed shaking into my lap, he'd been my biggest fan, my stout defender, and my reliable snuggle partner. Now, once Bethany scratched his head and got a few licks, he shook himself and waddled over to a tree stump to relieve himself.

"The woman who came by today? I've never met her before, and she wouldn't leave a name. But she was practically apoplectic." I smiled; even though "practically apoplectic" didn't sound promising, I did love Bethany's vocabulary. "She told me she absolutely needed to talk to you."

"Well, I'm here now," I said. "She can come find me."

"Right," Bethany said, but a cloud had passed over her bright face.

"What's wrong?" I asked.

"She said something about you stealing the store."

"Stealing the store?"

She shrugged. "I don't know what she meant. But I got the impression she's planning to instigate trouble."

"Fabulous," I said. "Well, what's a good story without a few plot twists?" This was part of my new goal, which was to look on the bright side and count my blessings. Some days were easier than others. "Speaking of stories, how's your mystery going?" I asked.

"I've gotten to the dead body," she said, "but now I'm kind of stuck. I put the book to the side until after the grand re-opening, though. I've got K. T. Anderson set up for a reading an hour after it starts, and I even talked the local paper into sending a reporter over tomorrow!"

K. T. Anderson was a Maine-based bestselling mystery author who had set an entire series in a town not far from here; getting her to come to the grand opening was a coup. "You are amazing, Bethany," I said, meaning every word.

"Happy to do it. Come see what I've done!"

Leaving my U-Haul trailer behind and feeling rather brighter, I followed my young assistant into Seaside Cottage Books, Winston trotting along at my heels.

The bright blue walls and white bookshelves were fresh and clean, the neatly stacked books like jewels just waiting to be plucked from the shelves. The window seat in the bay window at the front of the store was lined with my hand-made pillows, an inviting nook to tuck into with a book, and the armchairs tucked into the corners here and there gave the whole place the sweet, cozy feel I remembered from when I'd spent summer afternoons in the shop as a girl, when Loretta was still in good health. I walked from room to room, the gleaming wood floors creaking under my feet, and resisted the urge to pinch myself. Where the store, when I first took possession, had been dark and close, the windows covered over with old blankets and the rooms smelling of dust and must, over the past few months, Bethany and I had transformed it into a bright, clean space that smelled of lemon and new books and, above all, possibility.

"I set the table up here in the room with the local books, under the window," Bethany said, leading me to one of the front rooms. "I'm featuring K. T. Anderson's latest, of course. I didn't like it as much as the last one—it's a little heavy on the romance part—but it'll sell well. I ordered lots of stock for her to sign." Sure enough, a table with a light blue table-cloth sat along the wall, two coffee percolators and several platters waiting for the cookies I'd been stocking the freezer with for the last month. Prominently on shelves and tables around the store a stack of postcards was displayed that showed a picture of Seaside Books, including a 10% off coupon and the promo copy we'd come up with together —"Sink Your Teeth into a Good Book—Free Cookie with Every Purchase."

"It looks terrific," I said. "I don't know how I'll ever thank you."

"Become a booming success and feature my first book," Bethany said, "and we'll call it even."

"Of course," I said, grinning at her. I had total faith in Bethany; she was smart, enthusiastic, dedicated, and one of the hardest workers I knew.

I glanced around the store, which was picture-perfect and ready for opening, with pride and anticipation mixed with a little bit of anxiety. After all, everything was riding on this venture. I'd spent the last twenty years taking care of my daughters, running a home, and working part-time at one of Boston's independent bookstores, Bean Books. Now that I was single again, I needed to be able to take care of myself, and after being out of the workforce for two decades, my prospects in corporate America were rather limited. Besides, I couldn't envision spending the next twenty years in some oatmeal-colored cubicle answering phones and doing filing, which was pretty much the only option available for someone with my work experience.

With real estate prices in Boston, there was no way I could pay my rent with the salary that Ellie, the owner of Bean Books and a dear friend, was able to pay me, even though she had offered me an assistant manager position. When Ellie told me Loretta was ill and might be looking for someone to help run Seaside Cottage Books—or even take it over for her—something inside me responded. I'd always fantasized about owning my own bookstore and living in a small community, and I wasn't getting any younger. Did I really want my obituary to say "She always wanted to own a bookstore but never got around to it"? No matter what happened, I was glad I'd gone after what I'd always wanted; and Ellie had been a terrific cheerleader and consultant during my moments of doubt.

Winston seemed to approve of the new digs, too; he'd settled down into the dog bed I'd put beside the old desk I was using as a counter, looking content for the first time that day. Or at least relieved to be out of his crate. I knew the demand for dinner would be coming soon, though.

"Mail is in the top drawer of the desk—there were a few things that looked important, so I put them on top of the stack—and I shelved another order of books that came in today," Bethany informed me. "There was a new one from

Barbara Ross in the order, so I put it in the New Releases display."

"Perfect," I told her.

"I'm going to head home for dinner," she said. "But I'll be back tomorrow. If you need help unloading, I can ask my cousins to come give us a hand tomorrow morning."

"That would be a massive help; there's no way I could get that couch up the stairs on my own, much less the mattress. I can't thank you enough!"

"See you in the morning, then. I can't wait!"

"Text me when you get home, okay?'

"I will," she promised.

I watched through the front window as Bethany climbed onto her bike and turned right on Cottage Street, keeping my eyes on her until she disappeared from sight. Her house was only a few blocks away. I knew Snug Harbor was safe, but I also knew I wouldn't sleep soundly unless I knew Bethany had gotten home okay.

Once a mother, always a mother, I suppose.

"LET'S STRETCH OUR LEGS," I suggested, grabbing a leash from the passenger seat of the car and clipping it to Winston's collar. With a glance back at the house—and the U-Haul I still had to unload—we headed down the grassy trail to the water, pausing to inspect a few raspberry bushes with berries hidden under the yellow-green leaves, Winston straining at the leash and sniffing everything in range. Berries I would pick and put into ice cream sundaes, into muffins... I had so many things to look forward to this summer. Beach roses filled the air with their winey perfume, the bright blooms studding the dark green foliage.

Winston romped happily toward the water, smelling all the grass tufts, only slowing down and treading carefully when we got to the rocky beach. The tide was halfway out, and Winston was staying close beside me. Even though the waves in the harbor were minimal, he'd been swamped by a rogue wave once, and had had new respect for the ocean ever since. As we walked, I scanned the dark rocks mixed with flecks of brown seaweed, searching out of habit for sea glass. I found two brown chunks, doubtless the remains of old beer bottles; a couple of green shards; and two bits of delicate pale green that must have started life as Coke bottles; and I was about to turn back when a glint of cobalt caught my eye. I scooped it up and rinsed it off; it was a beautiful, deep blue shard, my favorite color and a lucky find. I tucked it in my pocket and walked up the beach, my stomach rumbling. What I really wanted to do was go to one of those restaurants up the street and indulge in a lobster dinner, but I was on a tunafish budget, so a homemade sandwich would have to do.

I grabbed the overnight case from the back seat of the SUV and climbed the back stairs to the apartment porch, Winston in my wake. Then I unlocked the door and stepped inside, flipping on the light with my elbow, and smiled. It was cozy, sweet, and... in a word, perfect.

In the back of the little house, with a gorgeous view of the harbor, was the living room, whose natural-colored floors and white walls (painted by me) looked fresh and bright, even in the evening. Although the furnishings currently consisted of nothing more than two folding chairs and a dust mop, I could picture how it would be once I brought in my white couch and coffee table, with a big blue rag rug against the golden floor.

The kitchen was small, but cozy, also with wood floors

and white walls, with a card table I'd gotten at the second-hand store in the corner. I'd outfitted the kitchen with odds and ends from my kitchen in Boston, including a toaster oven I'd been meaning to throw away for years, a coffeemaker that had been state-of-the-art in the late 1990s, and stacks of white and blue plates from Goodwill. I plopped down my overnight bag, released Winston from his leash, and grabbed a loaf of bread I'd put in the freezer the last time I was here, tucking two slices into the toaster oven and fishing in the small fridge for cheese. A bottle of cheap but not entirely undrinkable Prosecco sat in the fridge door; I'd bought it in anticipation of this night.

I slapped a slice of cheddar cheese on each piece of bread, then hit "toast" and retrieved a jam jar from the cabinet. While Winston watched, I popped the cork on the Prosecco and filled the jar. Then, jam jar in hand, I walked into the living room and surveyed the view from the kitchen window, which overlooked the harbor.

The sandbar connecting Snug Harbor to Snug Island had been almost swallowed up by the tide, and two late seagulls picked through the broken shells at the water's edge. Two sea kayakers were heading out from the island, paddling toward Snug Harbor, probably anxious to get back before total darkness fell. The sky was rose and peach and deep, deep, blue, and the first two stars twinkled in the cobalt swath of sky.

I looked down to where Winston stood behind me, looking up at me expectantly, head cocked to one side. "To new beginnings," I said, slipping my companion a piece of cheese before raising my jar in a toast, then sipping the fizzy Prosecco. "We made it."

As I spoke, I noticed a furtive figure slipping out of the trees and creeping up the path to the house. Then it paused, and I could see the pale oval of a face looking up at the lit window. As if whoever it was had changed their mind, he or she hustled back into the trees, melting into the shadows. Beside me, standing at the glass door, Winston's hackles rose, and he growled.

Goose bumps rose on my arms for the second time that night—this time, not in a good way. "It's okay," I reassured the little dog, hoping to reassure myself at the same time. "Whoever it is is gone."

As I spoke, the smell of burning toast filled the air. "Drat," I said, and I hurried back to the kitchen, where the edges of the toast had blackened.

I pulled it out of the toaster and onto a plate, burning myself in the process, and cut off the edges with a butter knife, then sat down at the table with my sad-looking toasted cheese sandwich and a jam jar of Prosecco, still wondering who had headed up the path and changed tack at the last minute.

Whoever it was was gone, I told myself as I bit into my sandwich. And I had other things to worry about.

Like unpacking the truck.

And preparing to have all of Snug Harbor descend on my fledgling bookstore in less than 24 hours.

IT WAS ALMOST midnight by the time I curled up with Winston snuggled into the crook of my arm. I hoped it was my last night sleeping on an air mattress, but with my crisp blue and white percale sheets, fluffy blanket, and soft pillows, it wasn't exactly a hardship. Besides, it was lovely being able to see the stars out my window; and to open the window and hear the lap of the water against the shore and the breeze in the maple tree next to the house, instead of Boston traffic in the distance.

I read one of Lee Strauss' charming Ginger Gold books until my eyes started to droop. Then I reached to turn off the lamp I'd set up next to the head of the mattress and burrowed into the covers, lulled to sleep by Winston's steady breathing and the soothing sound of the ocean.

Until a crashing sound from downstairs woke me up.

2

*W*inston and I jerked awake simultaneously, both sitting up in a near panic. Winston stood at attention, issuing short yippy, anxious barks. I shushed him, listening; sure enough, there was another clunk, from somewhere below me.

My thoughts sprang to the skulking figure I'd seen behind the shop earlier. Had someone broken in?

The moon had risen as I slept, illuminating the room enough so that I didn't need to turn on a light. I grabbed my bathrobe from the hook next to the door and wrapped it around me, tiptoeing toward the bedroom door. Winston watched from the mattress, no longer barking but whining anxiously. Evidently, he wasn't quite brave enough to join me.

I grabbed the dust mop, edged over to the door to the stairs, and took a deep breath. Then I unlocked the door, yanked it open, and turned on the light. "Is someone down there? I'm armed," I announced, stretching the truth just a tad.

There was a shuffling sound from downstairs, then footsteps. I caught a glimpse of movement; a moment later, I heard the back door creak open and slam shut.

I closed the apartment door and locked it, and hurried to the back windows. Sure enough, a flashlight bobbed down the path, right where I'd seen someone earlier that day. Winston joined me, growling quietly, as I watched it disappear. Then, still holding the dust mop, I unlocked the door and headed downstairs, Winston a safe ten steps behind me, still growling.

It was weird being in the store knowing someone had just left. I headed to the back door first; it was shut, but unlocked. I opened it; there was no splintering on the door frame, or any sign of forced entry. Did someone other than Bethany and me have a key? I wondered. When I'd bought the place from Loretta Satterthwaite, she'd turned over the keys, and I hadn't had the doors rekeyed. Maybe one of the former employees had a copy.

But why would they be breaking into the store?

At first glance, nothing looked any different than it had when Bethany and I walked through. The desk appeared untouched; nobody had been rifling through the drawers, thank goodness, and the table Bethany had set up in the front room was still pristine.

Something had fallen over, though. I'd heard it.

But what?

I found it in the back room.

Someone had dumped the books off one of the shelves Bethany and I had neatly organized in the Nature section and started to pry the back of the bookcase away from the wall.

If they were looking for a cavity of some sort, they were out of luck; the only thing behind the shelf was wallboard.

I touched the splintered wood of the bookshelf and

cursed under my breath, then stooped to retrieve the books that had been thrown to the floor—several were favorites by Rachel Carson and Bernd Heinrich. It bothered me that someone would treat books with such disregard, but I reminded myself to be thankful that the damage wasn't worse. A few had bent covers, but most were okay, and I replaced them carefully on the shelf. I'd have to get someone in to fix the back of the shelf, but thankfully the books covered the worst of it; there was only a small pulled-back area visible above the books on the left end of the shelf.

After I finished rearranging the shelf, I tapped around the other shelves, listening for a hollow sound, but heard nothing suspicious. Then I walked through the rest of the shop, tapping on walls, looking for more damage, and wondering why someone had broken into my shop to pull back a bookshelf.

Had they been looking for something hidden?

And if so, what?

THE NEXT DAY went by in a whirlwind. Bethany's cousins, Shane and Ernest, came by and helped me unload the U-Haul, leaving the formerly empty apartment riddled with boxes and furniture, including my bed, which I'd disassembled for the move and which now lay in pieces on the bedroom floor.

As Shane and Ernest manhandled a queen-sized mattress up the exterior stairs, I turned to Bethany, who was bundled up against the morning chill and sipping coffee out of a heavy pottery mug. "Have you had any issues with anyone breaking in?" I asked her.

"What?" she asked, her young brow furrowed. "Not that I know of... why?"

I related what had happened the night before.

"That's terrifying," she said. "Did you see who it was?"

"No," I said, "but whoever it was seemed to have a key; the back door was unlocked."

"I've had a few things move seemingly of their own accord the last few months, but I put that down to forgetfulness—or you being here when I wasn't. Nobody's taken a crowbar to anything, though. Are you sure the door was locked?" she asked. "It's easy to forget."

"I wish I could say I was," I admitted, "but I don't specifically remember actually locking it." I sighed. "I should probably have everything rekeyed." I didn't want to spend the money, but I didn't want to have to reassemble my bookshelves, either. I did a quick Google search on my phone, left a message for the first local locksmith that came up, and then started hauling boxes up the stairs.

The U-Haul was unloaded in record time, leaving me with a thicket of boxes to sort through. The apartment could wait, though; not only did I have to return the U-Haul, but there were still preparations to be done for the grand opening. As soon as Shane and Ernest left, each with an envelope of cash and some home-baked cookies, I headed out to drop off the U-Haul. It was almost 2:00 before I returned to the store. Bethany was already there, wearing an "I LOVE BIG BOOKS AND I CANNOT LIE" T-shirt and cleaning and setting up chairs she'd found in the storage shed out back; we'd need them for the author reading.

It was an hour before opening when I began putting out cookies and setting out cups and plates, satisfied that I'd gotten everything else about as clean and fresh as I could. Bethany was doing a few last-minute errands while I made the punch and set out the treats. When I had arranged the cookies—I'd included my favorite lemon bars, several dozen of my specialty double-chocolate-chip cookies, and three batches of jam thumbprints—added the last bottle of soda to the punch bowl and filled the percolators with ground coffee and water, I collapsed into the chair behind the big antique desk. Winston, who had spent the day busily running around supervising, sank into his dog bed beside me, looking exhausted. My eyes drifted to the top drawer; Bethany had said there were some important-looking letters in there, but I hadn't gotten around to looking at them yet. I was sure many of them were bills I should probably make myself face, even if that was the last thing on the planet I felt like doing right now. I sighed and steeled myself for what was in the drawer.

As I reached for the handle, there was a knock at the front door. I looked up in surprise to see my mother, her long gray hair swept up into a loose bun and a cheerful smile on her round face.

"Welcome to Snug Harbor, sweetheart!" she said, pulling me into a one-armed perfumed hug (the other hand was holding a bag) as I opened the door. My mother had a camp on Crescent Lake that she'd taken to staying in full-time a few years back; it was where I had spent many summers as a girl. My daughters had practically grown up there, spending every school vacation canoeing off the dock and catching fireflies, then coming in for root beer floats and jigsaw puzzles. Once Ted and I separated, I went on a week-long trip to the Gray Whale Inn on Cranberry Island, Maine, with my boss and old friend Ellie as I tried to figure out what to do next; it was there that I found out about Loretta's situation, and both Ellie and the delightful innkeeper, Natalie Barnes, encouraged me to look into taking over the store. I'd then spent a few weeks at my mother's camp, losing myself in the Agatha Christies that still lined the bookshelves, and drinking hot chocolate on the dock while reflecting on my new circumstances and trying to decide if becoming a bookstore owner was the right thing to do.

After a week of thinking, I'd ventured out to find Loretta, who told me that Seaside Cottage Books was indeed for sale, and that she'd love for me to take over the store. When she and I came to a number that almost exactly matched my settlement, it seemed like a sign from the universe that this was where the next chapter of my life was meant to unfold. My mother, of course, was delighted that I was relocating to Snug Harbor, although she hadn't yet come to terms with the fact that Ted and I were no longer married. I knew she fostered hopes that our expired marriage would one day be resuscitated.

"Thanks, Mom," I said as my mother released me from her scented hug.

"Here are some lemon cookies," she said, proffering a Tupperware container. "I figured you could use extra."

"Thank you!" I said.

"I made a batch of your favorite coconut cookies, too; they're in the back of the car. I'll go get them." She marched down the steps to where her green Subaru was parked, then opened the back door and pulled out a second big Tupperware container. "I thought I'd come early in case you need a little help," she said as she closed the car door and headed back up the walk to the store.

"Thanks," I said half-heartedly, trailing her up the porch steps and into Seaside Cottage Books.

She stopped as the door opened. "Oh, wow, Maxine." My mother was the only person on the planet who still called me Maxine; I'd been Max since junior high, and I preferred it that way. "The place looks terrific." Her eyes crinkled into a smile as she turned to me and said, tenderly, "Loretta would be thrilled."

"I just wish she were here to see it." Loretta had sold me the store in February, and had passed just a month ago, from pancreatic cancer. It was the diagnosis that had led her to sell the store.

"She'd be so proud of you," my mother told me, putting an arm around my shoulder again. "I know I am."

"I hope so," I replied, thinking of the bills that were likely piled up in the drawer—and that I hoped to soon be able to pay.

"By the way," she said as she popped open the Tupperware and began making a pile of her golden coconut cookies next to the lemon bars, "you'll never guess who else moved back to town!"

"Who?" I asked.

"Remember that boy you used to go out on the boat with? Nicholas Waters?"

"I do," I said with a pang. He'd been my first love, but it had ended badly. Very badly.

"Well, he's come back and set up shop as an attorney here in Snug Harbor."

I blinked. Nicholas Waters was ancient history in my book. I hadn't counted on him being back in town when I moved to Snug Harbor. Was I going to have to run into him every other day at the IGA? Was I going to encounter him on my daily walks, too? Was he going to be parading a wife or girlfriend all over the place, who I'd have to pretend not to be jealous of? I was surprised at the feelings that surged in my heart at the mention of his name; I'd thought he was no longer someone I cared about, but hearts have long memories. "Have you seen him?" I asked, trying to sound casual.

"No. I only know because Sadie at the library told me the other day. She knew you two used to be close; she thought it was a funny coincidence, you both moving to town within a month of each other."

Lucky me. I was dying to ask about five thousand questions. Like, was he married? Had he gained 100 pounds? Did he still have his hair? But my mother hadn't seen him, just heard about him. And the last thing I wanted was for her to know I still cared about Nicholas.

In fact, it bothered *me* to find out how much I still cared about Nicholas. If only Scooter Dempsey hadn't spread those rumors about me all those years ago...

I pushed the thought from my mind. It had all happened a long time ago. And if I hadn't met and married Ted, I wouldn't have Audrey and Caroline, the two lights of my life. Best to let it lie.

"The cookies look terrific," I said, changing the subject. "I figure we'll start the coffee makers about a half hour before showtime. Our star author should be here any moment. In the meantime, if you want to help, I forgot to bring down the napkins; there's a bag upstairs in the kitchen. If you could bring those down and put them on the table, that would be wonderful."

"Will do," she said, and bustled up the stairs to retrieve them.

I straightened my blouse a little—I'd chosen to wear a starched white cotton button-down with a sea glass necklace in blues and greens, along with capri-length skinny jeans and wedge sandals—and attempted to give the impression of a prosperous bookstore owner. I caught a glimpse of myself reflected in the store's side window. Dark hair, still long down my back, pulled up in a clip. Hazel eyes that were only a little bit puffy from my little crying binge, arched, dark brows, a long, straight nose, and a roundish face that looked a little like my mother's. I had to admit I looked pretty good. Even if there was a little extra real estate under the blouse at the moment. I was adjusting my blouse when there was a knock at the door

I turned to see who it was, and smiled when I recognized K. T. Anderson. She didn't look exactly like her author photo—no one ever does—but it was a close likeness, and I could tell already that I preferred her smile in person. I hurried over to the door and opened it, and my face froze.

Next to the author, his arm linked with hers, stood my ex-husband.

3

*T*ed and I stared at each other for what felt like a decade before I recovered myself. I grabbed at the doorknob and yanked the door open, my face still in a rictus of a smile.

"Hello," I said in a strangled-sounding voice.

"I'm K. T. Anderson—Kirsten," announced the author. She was an attractive woman a few years older than me with streaked red hair and a knee-length skirt that showed off her shapely calves. "Are you Bethany?"

"Max," I gurgled, automatically holding out a hand for her to shake.

"Max? Oh, yes... she mentioned you were the store owner. This is my boyfriend Theodore," she said cheerfully. I glanced over at my ex-husband, whose face had gone pale.

"We've met," I informed her.

"Oh, really? Small world!" she said in a bright voice.

She had no idea, I thought as I stared at my husband's familiar form.

"What a lovely store you have; thank you so much for

inviting me." She paused as I continued to stare, then added, "May we come in?"

"Of course," I said. "I'm so sorry; please do. Can I get you a bottle of water, or something to drink?" I asked, trying to sound pleasant and inviting despite the fact that I felt as if I'd been hit by a tractor trailer. I avoided looking at Ted as I chirped, "We've got cookies, too."

"A bottle of water would be lovely, but I'll skip the cookies," she said, patting her flat stomach. "I'm trying to lose a few pounds!"

I nodded and pulled my blouse out a bit, hoping it wasn't molding too closely to my recently expanded waistline. I was overly conscious of Ted's presence as Kirsten's eyes roved over the interior of the store. "This is a gorgeous little place; it looks like it belongs in a book itself. Thank you so much for inviting me to the opening; it's an honor!"

"I'm so glad you could come," I said, my eyes straying to Ted, who was studiously avoiding my eyes.

There was maybe a little more white at the temples than I remembered, and he had thinned out a bit, but other than that he was exactly the same as he had been for the two decades we were married. He even smelled the same; I caught a whiff of his Old Spice as he followed Kirsten around the room.

"Oooh, these cookies do look tempting," Kirsten said, distracting me from my assessment of my former husband.

"Help yourself if you change your mind," I said. "My mother made the coconut ones on the front."

"I thought those looked familiar," Ted said. "I've missed those."

"You've had her mother's cookies?" Kirsten said, eyeing her beau. "You must know each other pretty well, then. How *do* you know each other, anyway?"

"Ah, Maxine is my, uh, ex-wife," Ted said, a familiar flush starting at the collar of his button-down shirt and moving up to his temples.

Maxine. Ted had never called me that. Then again, I had never called him Theodore.

"Wait. What?" Kirsten looked back and forth between Ted and me. "You knew this was her store?"

"No!" he protested. "I had no idea. We've been living apart for months, and we've kind of... well, not talked a whole lot."

"You've been busy," I said, nodding toward Kirsten.

"Right," he said, his face turning beet colored. "I've been to Snug Harbor before, of course... but I didn't know Max... Maxine was the one who bought the store. You told me you were talking to someone named Bethany."

"Bethany's my right-hand woman," I explained. "She's been organizing most of the opening for me."

Kirsten blinked her long lashes. "So you had no idea this was your ex-wife's shop until we got to the front door."

"No," Ted and I said in unison.

She started laughing, a slightly braying laugh that made me feel a little bit better. She wasn't totally perfect, thank heavens. "This is just too good," she said. "I'm going to have to use this in a book someday." She eyed me. "Max, eh? I feel like I know you already."

"Really?" I asked, darting a look at Ted, who had turned, against all probability, an even darker shade of red.

"Yup. You eat a bowl of oatmeal with banana and a spoonful of peanut butter almost every morning. You have a stack of books beside your bed about two feet high, and more on the night stand. You love mysteries and travel books the most, but you read just about everything. You've always dreamed of owning a bookstore, you adopted a little dog six years ago from the pound, you take baths before bed most nights, and refused to make an offer on two houses because they only had showers." She squinted at me. "And Audrey takes after you. A lot. In fact, I can't believe I didn't make the connection."

"Wait... you know Audrey?"

"Of course," she said.

I swallowed hard, uncomfortable with how much Ted had shared with her. What else did she know about me? And, most importantly, why hadn't Ted consulted me before introducing this new woman to our daughters? I tried to make eye contact with my ex-husband, but he was staring at the ceiling, evidently entranced by the recent paint job. I turned back to Kirsten. "You've met our daughters?" I asked.

"Oh, loads of times," Kirsten said. "We took them to dinner just last week." That must have been while I was clearing the last of the stuff out of our formerly shared house, I thought. I raised my eyebrows at Ted.

My ex-husband cleared his throat, now studying the floorboards. "I, uh, was going to talk to you about it..."

"A bit late now," I pointed out. I was a little hurt; I'd talked with them at least once a week, and neither of them had mentioned that Ted had a girlfriend. Their dad and I had only been officially divorced for eight months; maybe they were trying to shield me from the pain? I didn't know, but I was definitely going to bring it up soon.

"I gave Audrey a book of mine to read a few weeks ago; I can't wait to hear what she thinks of it. Like I said, I know you favor mysteries and travel writing, but I've been introducing her to some more literary work."

I resisted the urge to bean her with an Agatha Christie compendium and pasted on a polite smile. "You seem to know all about me," I said to Kirsten, "but Ted's never even mentioned you to me."

"No?" she asked.

"Not a word," I confirmed. "How did you two meet, anyway?"

Kirsten beamed up at Ted, and a dreamy look crossed her face as she turned back to me. "About six months ago, he came to a reading I did, in Boston."

Six months. When the ink on the divorce decree had barely dried. I turned and stared at Ted. "A book reading?" I asked. My ex-husband hadn't attended a single literary event in the 22 years I'd known him.

He shrugged, a sheepish look on his face. "It looked interesting."

"Oh, he was a great audience member. He'd read the whole book, asked the most interesting questions... and even invited me out for a cocktail afterwards. We hit it off immediately, and we've been inseparable ever since. We've been to Greece and Italy, and we're planning a month-long tour of Eastern Europe in the spring."

I stared at the stranger to whom I'd been married for two decades. Attending author events in his spare time? A month-long tour of Europe? Inseparable? Ted had been a workaholic as long as I'd known him. Getting him home to dinner before eight had taken either an act of God or a promise of chicken and dumplings and possibly apple pie, his absolute favorite dinner. I could barely get him to take a weekend off to visit Snug Harbor, much less spend a month across the Atlantic. And now he was accompanying this woman to weekend readings and spending all his spare time with her?

And why was she telling me all this, anyway?

"I've got a few more things to take care of," I informed the happy couple, forcing a pleasant expression and trying not to look as upset as I was. "Help yourselves to snacks; I'll be back in a few minutes."

Without waiting for an answer, I turned and fled up the stairs to my apartment, where I sank down in the welter of boxes and burst into tears.

~

I ALLOWED myself a good five-minute breakdown before telling myself it was time to pull it together. I was sitting between two boxes marked "mystery books," wiping my eyes and giving myself a pep talk, when there was a knock on the apartment door. It couldn't be Ted... er, Theodore... could it?

"Max?"

I was relieved to recognize Bethany's voice. "Come in," I said, doing a last tear-swipe.

"It's almost time to open the front..." She rounded a stack of boxes and spotted me, and broke off mid-sentence. "What happened?"

"What do you mean?" I asked.

"Your face is all... blotchy."

"It's nothing," I said, clambering to my feet. My face always got mottled when I cried. Hopefully a good splash of cold water would make it less apparent.

"Balderdash," she said. "Something's wrong. Did the paper not run the announcement about the opening? Did you hear something bad from the bank?"

"No," I said. "Nothing like that."

"What, then?"

"You know the man with the author?"

"Theodore?" she asked. "He seems very nice; I just met him."

I took a deep breath. "I always knew him as Ted. He's my ex-husband."

"He's your... what?" Bethany blinked. "K. T. Anderson's boyfriend is your ex-husband? But didn't you just divorce, like a few months ago?"

"Eight."

"Still, that's, like, practically yesterday. What is he doing here? That's so thoughtless!"

"He didn't know," I said. "When she was setting up the book talk, Kirsten only talked with you, not me. And we've been taking a break from each other, so he had no idea I'd bought the shop."

"Oh, man... I'm so sorry I invited her," Bethany said. "It's just her last book hit the New York Times list, and it's set in Maine, and I thought... "

"You did the right thing," I reassured her. "It's the right thing for the shop, and there was no way to know. But now," I said, "it's time to face the music. The show must go on. Or something like that." I touched my face again. "As soon as I get rid of the blotchiness, that is."

"I'll go down and get her situated while you do what you have to do," Bethany said. "I'll do the author-wrangling if you'll schmooze. Are you sure you'll be all right?"

"Right as rain," I lied, wondering if I was going to be reduced to communicating in idioms for the rest of the day. At least the day can't get any worse, I told myself as I hurried to the small bathroom and turned on the cold water tap.

Sadly, I was dead wrong.

4

*T*rue to her word, Bethany handled Kirsten and Ted for me as I finished a few last-minute chores, such as sweeping the front porch, figuring out how to turn on music, and starting the coffee pots.

It was ten minutes to opening when my mother reappeared. "Not much of a crowd, is there?" she commented as I let her in the door.

"We're not open for another ten minutes," I pointed out. "But Ted is here. Although he goes by Theodore now, apparently."

"Ted? Awww. That was so nice of him. He still cares for you, you know," she said, and patted my cheek. "It's so good of him to support you!"

"He's not here to support me. He's here with his girl-friend. The author." I pointed to the sign on the table with the glamour shot of K. T. Anderson front and center. Her cheekbones looked like someone had sculpted them with a chisel, and her lips were as full as a twelve-year-old's. I resisted the urge to make some alterations with a Sharpie. "Apparently they're taking a trip to Europe soon."

She blinked at me. "What? Ted never wanted to go to Europe before."

"He does now. And he goes to literary readings these days, too, apparently."

My mother's face softened into a sad look that threatened to make me cry a little again. "Oh, honey, I'm so sorry."

"Thanks. I'm glad he's happy," I said staunchly.

And I was. Our marriage had died a slow, inexorable, natural death, crushed under the strain of day-to-day-living and divergent growth, and although both of us were torn up when it ended, we were also a little relieved to no longer have to live with the constant tension. But it stung to think that the things I'd wanted in our marriage for so long were suddenly on offer to someone else. A glamorous bestselling author, no less.

Who was doing a reading in my store with her adoring boyfriend looking on in just a few minutes.

"You never know. He could come back," my mother attempted to reassure me.

"Mom, I know you're trying to help, but we parted ways for a reason. I want to be friends with him, and share parenting our daughters, but our relationship..." I trailed off.

"You never know!" she repeated, then, at a slitty-eyed look from me, thankfully dropped it. "Anyway. Where is he? I'd like to say hi."

"On the back porch," I said in a voice that sounded surly even to me.

"Are you sure it's okay if I say hi?"

"It's fine," I said flatly.

At five minutes before the opening, I turned the sign to OPEN and said a little prayer.

At three minutes before the opening, I began to worry.

At two minutes before the opening, I began to panic.

And then, just as the minute hand on my watch turned to 12, about twenty people materialized on the sidewalk in front of the store and trickled onto the store's front porch.

I threw open the door and welcomed them, trying not to look as relieved as I felt, and within fifteen minutes, the little store was full of locals and tourists, browsing bookshelves and plowing through the cookies and coffee.

"I told you it would be fine," Bethany murmured as she drifted in to check up on things. "Free food works every time."

"How's Kirsten?" I asked.

"She and... well, I set them up on the back porch for now, and your mother's there, too," she said. "We're already running out of cookies... I'll go refill them."

"Thanks," I said, and turned to greet another customer.

When we were five minutes from the start of the reading, the chairs had all filled up and folks were standing on the edges of the room. I was edging back toward the front door when someone tapped me on the shoulder. I turned around to face a handsome man about my age, with salt-and-pepper hair, high cheekbones, and very familiar brown eyes.

"Max? Is that you?"

"Nicholas?" I blinked.

"That's me," he said. "A bit grayer than I was," he said. "You look just the same, though."

"No," I said, flushing. "Two kids and a lot of years have taken their toll."

"Married, then?" he asked, and I thought I caught a flash of disappointment.

"No," I said. "Well, not anymore. You?"

"Never married," he said. "Came close a few times, but it never clicked." He gave me a familiar grin that made my heart turn over; some things hadn't changed. "You never said what you're doing here. Are you in town visiting your mom?"

"No... I bought the book store!"

"What?" he asked. "I thought someone named Maxine Sayers bought it..."

"That's me," I said. "Married name."

"No one ever calls you Maxine!" he said.

"Except my mother and attorneys on legal documents," I said.

"No wonder!" he told me. "I just don't see you as a Maxine, though." Something about the way he said my name made me feel warm and tingly inside; there seemed to have been something of a thaw over the intervening decades. I was trying to come up with a response when Bethany touched my elbow. "It's about time to do the introduction," she advised me.

"Excuse me," I told Nicholas, feeling my heart fluttering a bit. "I've got to go introduce the author... I'd love to catch up more after the reading!"

"I'd like that, actually," he said, again flashing me that smile that hadn't changed in... well, let's just say a lot of years.

I stepped up to the front of the room and faced the crowd; it wasn't exactly standing-room-only at Seaside Cottage Books, but the place was pleasantly full. I just hoped everyone wasn't here only for the free food. I tugged at the hem of my blouse a little self-consciously and smiled at the audience.

"Thank you so much for coming to the grand re-opening

of Seaside Cottage Books. I know you all miss Loretta—I do, too—but I'll try to carry the torch as best I can. The bookstore always meant so much to me growing up, and I'm honored to carry on the tradition. It's so good to be back in Snug Harbor... I hope to catch up with those of you I know from way back" — I smiled at Nicholas, who grinned back at me— "and I'm looking forward to meeting everyone else. I hope the store will be a place you can come to relax, enjoy browsing, and find wonderful new authors. And speaking of authors..."

I launched into a description of our guest author with an enthusiasm I didn't quite feel, even though I'd enjoyed her romantic suspense books set a few hours down the coast in Portland, and tried not to look at her—or Ted, who was sitting in a chair next to her, holding her hand.

Instead, I scanned the room, finding my eyes drawn to Nicholas, of course, but seeing a number of other faces that looked vaguely familiar, along with several I didn't know. One woman in a short, pink dress sat in the front row, wearing big sunglasses despite the indoor, evening situation. She had long, straight, highlighted hair caught up in a French twist, and reminded me a bit of Audrey Hepburn. Sitting beside her was a woman who was almost the complete opposite; she looked as if she'd been born with a broom handle where her spine should be. Her entire affect was regal, from her cropped salt-and-pepper hair to her aquiline nose to the understated pearls ringing her neck. Had they come together? I wondered, and my gaze wandered on, stopping short when they reached a familiar visage I had hoped never to see again.

I forgot what I was saying for a moment. Scooter Dempsey smirked as I recovered myself; I got the distinct impression he knew exactly what I'd been thinking, and that that had been his intent.

"Sorry about that; I lost my train of thought there for a moment," I said. "As I was saying..." I finished the introduction and sat down as Kirsten took the stage, feeling a familiar old anger bubble up. Not at Kirsten, although I have to say I was less than thrilled with the fact that my stodgy ex-husband had suddenly discovered unplumbed depths with her that he would have scoffed at had I suggested them. I was mad at Scooter Dempsey. It was because of him that Nicholas had broken up with me all those years ago. I'd turned him down for a date, and he'd then spread rumors about me that I'd never been able to discredit. I'd never been able to forgive him. Would he do it again, now that I had the store?

Put it out of your head, I told myself. We weren't in high school anymore. We were all adults. And that was ancient history—history that needed to be put to bed.

I had just turned to focus on Kirsten again when she said, "Imagine my surprise when I found out the owner of this wonderful store is my boyfriend's ex-wife!"

There was a silence as she gestured toward me, and every set of eyes in the room fastened on me with prurient interest.

Including Nicholas's, which was not exactly the way I wanted to make my debut in Snug Harbor.

"He has good taste in women, doesn't he?" Kirsten continued, smiling in a way I imagine she thought was generous. I glanced at Ted, whose face was set in a stiff smile, his neck and cheeks flushed red yet again, and I prayed that the day would be over soon.

"At least it should be good for business," Bethany whispered from next to me. "Everyone likes... well... a personal interest story."

Uh huh.

I felt my own cheeks flaming and sneaked a glance at Nicholas, who was looking from me to Ted with raised eyebrows. A moment later, thankfully, Kirsten launched into her reading—a suspenseful bit involving a woman being held hostage on a bridge. Which at the moment sounded almost preferable to my current situation.

THE AUDIENCE THRONGED Kirsten after the reading, which was good for business—the stack of brightly colored books Bethany had placed next to her were being signed and handed to customers in large numbers. Bethany stood beside the author while I hurried to the register and began ringing up my first sales, trying very hard not to look at the glamour shot of K. T. Anderson, which was challenging, since it was the entire back cover. There was no sign of Nicholas, alas, and I hoped he stayed until the crowd cleared. I kept sneaking glances at Ted and Kirsten; he was beaming, looking like he'd won the top prize at the State Fair, and I found myself clenching my jaw.

I had just rung up a three-book purchase when I looked up to see Scooter. One of Kirsten's books was in his hand, along with what looked like a first-edition hardback Dick Francis mystery featuring a stylized horse and jockey on the cover, but he didn't hand the books to me.

"I had no idea you were the owner of the store these days," he said.

"Well, I am."

"Good to see you after all this time," he said with a faint smirk. "Did you receive a letter recently?'

"I haven't checked my mail the last day or two," I said, trying to disguise my distaste.

"You probably should," he said, the smirk broadening into a satisfied little smile that edged across his face.

I'd never liked Scooter, from the time I'd found him teasing Donny Knee, who had a speech impediment. I had been twelve, and several of us kids were hanging out, eating chocolate bars and slurping down sodas on the town playground. Donny had been trying to tell us about a fish he caught, but kept getting stuck on the F. Donny was turning red with frustration when Scooter had crumpled up his Snickers' bar wrapper and started mimicking him cruelly.

"What was that, Donny-boy? It was a f-f-f-f-f-f-? I've never heard of one of those."

Donny, embarrassed, tried again.

"A what?" Scooter teased.

"Stop it," I'd told him. Scooter was two years older than me, but I was always scrappy, and I hated seeing people teased. "Go on, Donny."

The stutter was worse now. He tried again, but could barely even get the "f" out.

"Retard," Scooter muttered.

"What did you call him?" I asked.

"Retard," he repeated. Tears formed in Donny's eyes, and he stopped even trying to talk.

I'd walked up to Scooter, who was six inches taller than me and had about forty pounds on me, but I didn't care. "Stop being a jerk."

"Who's gonna make me?" he'd asked, giving me that slitty-eyed little smile of his.

"If you don't leave him alone and get out of here, I'm

going to punch you in the nose," I'd told him, anger eliminating all traces of common sense.

He'd blinked, then started laughing. I didn't think; I just pulled back my right arm and popped him in the nose.

He'd dropped his Coke, and his hands flew to his nose. A trickle of blood leaked out between his fingers.

"You little..."

For a moment I'd thought he was going to punch me back, and the gravity of what I'd done swept over me, along with the first burst of fear. My whole body tensed, and I was ready to turn and run. He lowered his right hand, and my hands went up instinctively, shielding my face. But instead of hitting me, he turned and ran out of the playground, still holding his nose. Donny, my friend Denise, and I stared at his red jacket as it billowed out behind him, not quite sure we could believe what had just happened.

"It was a foot-long fish," Donny said totally clearly. "And thanks for doing that."

"Yeah," Denise chimed in. "You're a rock star; I can't believe you popped him in the nose!"

"Me neither," I said, my knees suddenly weak. "I need to sit down." I sank to the ground. What had I been thinking?

"What a jerk," Denise said, her fiery hair a halo around her face, backlit by the sun. "Let's get out of here before he changes his mind and comes back."

We left in a hurry, and Scooter had never brought it up with me again. But from that point forward, he'd done everything in his power to make my life difficult.

Including now. He had several decades and a few dozen more pounds on him, and maybe a little less hair on top of his head, but that face was unmistakably the same. Giving me that same slitty-eyed smile, he said, "You know you don't really own the store."

"Pardon me?" I asked.

"Loretta Satterthwaite didn't have the right to sell it. You may have bought her half, but her sister Agatha never signed over her part of it." He looked around at the people, the freshly painted walls, the books lined up neatly on the shelves. "So no matter how much you paid for it, none of this is really yours."

5

"*W*hat? That can't be right," I said, staring at him. "Loretta signed some kind of deed... I think it was called a quitclaim deed?" We'd done the transaction without real estate agents to make the process faster and less expensive, and I'd bought the store outright.

He shook his head. "Quitclaim deeds can be trouble. Too bad you didn't have a title search done."

"Yes," announced a large man, who had what a friend of mine called a "success belly" and the air of someone who's spent his whole life expecting things to fall into his lap and actually having it happen. "And it looks like you've done some renovations, too. Do you have permits for that?"

"Permits?" I croaked.

"Permits," he repeated. "I understand some of your paperwork is out of date, and there's some question as to whether you're operating the business illegally." His mouth was a grim line in his flaccid face, but his eyes crinkled slightly; it was obvious he was more than happy to deliver this news. He lowered his voice and leaned forward conspiratorially, his jowls jiggling as he spoke. "Although maybe we can make a deal."

"A deal?" I asked. "Pardon me, but have we met?"

He blinked. "I thought you knew; I just won the selectman position in Snug Harbor. Cal Parker," he said, reaching out a beefy hand. I reached out to shake it, and ended up with my arm nearly wrenched out of the socket as he squeezed my hand and jerked it up and down a few times, then patted it with his other hand, making it look as if the end of my arm had been swallowed by some fleshy creature. "Let's talk later on," he said conspiratorially, but I couldn't help notice that half the people in line were leaning forward and listening. Not exactly what I'd dreamed about for my grand opening. "Maybe we can work something out," he suggested, and as he spoke, I could smell something fermented on his breath.

"Work something out?" I asked, prying my hand out of his grasp and feeling my stomach twist. I was out of money, and the last thing I wanted to do was make a back-room deal with a councilman. Was that what he was suggesting?

I turned to Scooter, who was watching the exchange between us with a smug smile. "Even if part of the house does still belong to Agatha Satterthwaite—which I don't believe—what do you have to do with it?"

"She was planning to sell the property to my company," he said. "For fair market value. Which, considering this is waterfront property, is likely considerably more than what Loretta charged you."

I glanced at the line of customers, many of whom had their ears perked up as they waited to pay. Loretta had really wanted me to have the store, and I hadn't researched the number we agreed on, but I knew it was low. I suddenly felt very tired, and a little bit sick. Had I just spent my life savings on a bum deal?

"Let's talk about this later," I said. "I've got a line of customers."

"Here's my card," the councilman said, producing one from his back pocket. I glanced at it briefly and shoved it next to the register.

"Thanks," I said. "I'll be in touch."

Cal gave Scooter the briefest of nods as he sauntered off, glad-handing anyone who came within range. I couldn't help but notice that he didn't seem very popular; a few people seemed to move intentionally out of his way.

Scooter was still standing in front of me, and I turned to him, ready to ring up his purchase; there was a long line, after all. "I'll ring that up," I offered.

"On second thought, I've changed my mind about the books." He tossed them down on the desk in front of me. "I have a better first edition at home," he said, pointing to a dinged corner that I would swear hadn't been there five minutes ago. "Good luck," he added, and waltzed out of the store, leaving me cold as ice and feeling like this time, *he* had just walloped *me* in the nose.

"Is everything okay?" asked the next customer, the woman in the pink dress, as I gathered the two books and tucked them behind the counter. One of them was now damaged, and the other—signed to Scooter, presumably—was now unsellable.

I shook myself and put on a smile. "Fine," I lied as she handed me the books.

"Cal and Scooter are both a piece of work," she said, lowering her sunglasses to watch him leave. "I can't believe Cal won the election. In fact, I can't believe nobody's killed him in self-defense yet."

"Thanks for being supportive," I said as I rang her up. I noticed the last name on her card was the same as the councilman's. "Gretchen Parker," I said, reading her credit card. "Are you two related?" I asked.

"Ex-wife," she said.

"Ah. I understand," I told her.

She glanced toward Ted and grinned at me. "I know you do. We women have to stick together, don't we? See you around... and don't let the jerks get you down," she said, tucking the book into her oversized purse and heading for the door before I could answer.

The next few customers stared at me with curiosity and complimented me on the bookstore, but didn't mention my ex-husband, thankfully. Until I got to the regal woman who had been seated next to Gretchen Parker.

"You'll want to watch out for Cal Parker," she advised me in a husky voice, looking toward the front door, through which the freshly minted selectman had exited a few minutes earlier. "He's a snake."

"I gathered," I said. "How is he involved with Scooter Dempsey?"

"They're in business together, at least unofficially," she said. "Cal bought the spot on the council and is using Snug Harbor to line his pockets. He beat me by two votes at the last election. I'm going after my seat again next time, but we'll have to do what we can to protect the town in the meantime."

"I'm so sorry," I said. "He seems like..."

"A jerk?" she asked as I rang up her sale.

"Exactly," I said.

"Welcome to Snug Harbor, by the way," she told me. "I'm Meryl Ferguson, and I'm glad you took over the store. Loretta told me she was delighted you were going to carry on the tradition; we were long-time friends. If there's anything I can do to help, let me know."

"Thanks," I said, warmed by the greeting. "It's good to meet you."

"Thanks for the book," she said as I handed her back *Fast Money*. "I'm sure I'll be seeing much more of you."

"I hope so," I said with honesty; I'd only just met Meryl, but I liked her. And she certainly seemed a better choice for Snug Harbor's council than the slimy Cal Parker.

"Hey," said the next person in line; a woman about my age, with a mass of dark hair around her face. "Nice presentation, particularly considering the circumstances." She leaned her head toward my ex-husband, who was still hovering behind our guest author. Her energetic voice was familiar somehow. "I noticed you chatting with Scooter Dempsey; how do you know him?" she asked.

"When I was twelve, I punched him in the nose for teasing Donny Knee about not being able to say 'fish.'"

"Wait." She blinked. "Are you Max Finnegan?"

"That's me, yes," I said, confused. "Or it was. My last name is Sayers now."

"It's me, Denise," she said. "I remember you doing it. It's one of my all-time favorite memories."

"Denise Wilmington?" I looked up at her, and suddenly I realized why her voice sounded familiar. "But your hair..." The Denise I remembered had been a flaming redhead.

She laughed. "I put a temporary color in it, just for fun. I'm still a ginger."

"Wow. You look good either way. I'm so glad to see you!" I said, still clutching the book. "I had no idea you were still in town!"

"I manage Sea Beans," she told me.

"The coffee shop down on Main Street?"

"That's the one," she said.

"I can't believe it," I said, my spirits rising a little bit at the encounter with an old friend. We'd been inseparable those summers in Snug Harbor, but had lost touch after that time had ended. "I'm so glad you're here. We'll have to catch up!"

She glanced behind her at the line. "I should probably let you ring up your customers, but I'd love that. I've got to go home and get dinner for the kids, but are you around tomorrow?"

"All day," I said.

"I'll bring some coffee after the morning shift, and we can catch up!"

"I'd love that," I said, feeling my heart expand. I finished the transaction and handed her the book. "Thank you so much for coming."

"The pleasure was all mine," she said, eyes sparkling. "See you tomorrow, okay?"

"I can't wait."

6

I spent the next hour at the register, too busy to think too much about the contested deed or the permits or my ex-husband or Scooter Dempsey. Well, almost too busy. Sales were remarkably good that first night; we moved a lot of Kirsten's books, along with a smattering of other books, mainly from the front display table Bethany had put together, and I asked Kirsten to sign stock so that we could continue featuring her books for folks who couldn't make it to her reading. As uncomfortable as it was knowing that she was my ex-husband's girlfriend, I was grateful to her, and I couldn't say I disliked her.

Although I wasn't going to come out and say I liked her, either.

"This was so fun!" she gushed as she signed a book, looking up at me from long-lashed eyes. Ted stood a few feet behind her, looking like he wasn't sure what to do, and my mother was watching all of us as she pretended to rearrange napkins on the snack table. Bethany had just dished out the last of the punch to a few stragglers and had promised to take over the register until close. "I think you're going to have a great little business here," Kirsten said. "Theodore tells me you're interested in writing mysteries, too!"

I glanced at him with a stiff smile. What hadn't he told her about me? "I've thought about it," I confessed.

"Well, you absolutely should. I know it never seems like the right time, but you just have to dive in there, you know? I mean, just like you did with the store here, and look how well that's turning out!"

Considering the conversation I'd had with Cal Parker a few hours earlier, I wasn't so sure how well it was turning out, but I wasn't going to share that with Kirsten. "I'll think about it," I said.

"You should start a mystery writing group. That's how I got my start in the business. It would be fun, and bring people into the store, too!"

I hated to admit it was a good idea, but it was. "You may be right," I admitted. "I'll talk to Bethany about setting something up."

Kirsten finished signing the last book with a flourish and added it to the stack. "I know the bookstore is about to close for the evening, and I was wondering: would you like to join Theodore and me for dinner? I feel like I already know you, but I'd love it if we could be friends."

I stole a glance at Ted, who looked like he'd rather spend a few quality minutes in an electric chair than go to dinner with his ex-wife and his new girlfriend. I shared the sentiment, so I declined. "Thanks for the offer, but I'm so wiped out from the launch that I think I'm going to clean up, take a bath, and collapse in bed." I smiled at her. "I appreciate it, though, and enjoyed meeting you. Thanks again for coming out; it really made a big difference."

"My pleasure. Anytime!" she said, getting up and

smoothing out her tight skirt. "Theodore, do you have my bag?"

"Right here," he said, producing it like a dutiful Sherpa. He'd done the same for me so many times over the years. And now he never would again. The grief shot through me again, suddenly, taking my breath away, realizing that what we had for so long, as imperfect as it was, was finished now.

"Well, we're off. Theodore tells me that the Lobster Thermidor at the Chart House is divine. If you change your mind..."

"Thanks," I said, "but perhaps another time."

"Of course," she responded. "Thanks again. And it's a beautiful little store you've got; I wish you all the success in the world."

"Likewise," I said feebly.

"Good to see you," Ted said awkwardly, then walked over and gave me a wooden-feeling hug. He still smelled like Old Spice and Tide laundry detergent, and again, the smell brought back a cascade of memories and feelings. "Take care of yourself," he said.

"You too," I told him, and watched them walk out of the store, Ted holding the door for his new flame. They were halfway down the front walk before he reached for her hand and squeezed it.

"That certainly was a grand opening," my mother said, putting a hand on my shoulder; she'd joined me without my noticing. "Are you doing okay?"

"Not exactly," I confessed. I told her what Cal Parker had said, and her eyes widened.

"Oh, Maxine. That's not good news. What are you going to do about it?"

Find someone more supportive to talk to, for starters, I

thought but didn't say. "I should probably look at the letter he said he sent."

"Probably," she said. "But you can't do anything about it tonight. Why don't you look at it first thing in the morning? And if you need an attorney, I understand Nicholas specializes in real estate law."

"That's right," I said.

"I saw you talking with him tonight," she commented. "I always thought he was a cute boy when you were a kid, but now he's a handsome man."

"He is," I agreed.

"I'd still love it if you and Ted got back together, of course," she said. "Not right now, obviously, but once the glamour of being with a gorgeous author wears off, I'm sure he'll realize how much he misses you."

Wow. I didn't even bother responding. "We should probably get the rest of the cookies cleaned up," I said, changing the subject.

"I don't think there are any left to clean up," my mother said. "They just loved my coconut cookies. I'll leave you the recipe if you like."

"Thanks," I said mechanically.

I spent the next hour cleaning up. People had managed to stash napkins and plates in the most interesting places; a few children had liberally decorated *Blueberries for Sal* and *Make Way for Ducklings* with crumbs and spilled punch, and the antique flatiron I used as a doorstop had somehow vanished into thin air. I got things in as good order as I could before I gave up, double-checked that all the doors and windows were locked, then grabbed the letters I'd been avoiding from the desk and retreated to my box-infested quarters above the shop.

There were several ads, a few bills, and two letters I dreaded opening.

Still, I had to face them, so I took a deep breath and opened the first envelope. It was from Board of Selectmen of the Town of Snug Harbor, telling me that it had come to the town's attention that I had done renovations without permits and that I would need to have the place inspected if I wanted to continue doing business. The deadline? Two weeks, or else I'd have to shut down the shop and/or pay hefty fines. Cal Parker hadn't been making that up, alas.

The other was from Scooter Dempsey, Esq., who evidently had managed to somehow get a law degree in addition to putting together a development company since last we'd met. The letter was on behalf of Agatha Satterthwaite, and informed me that the property did, in fact, not belong to me, and that I would need to reimburse Agatha for half of its appraised value I planned to continue doing business. He then went on to suggest that a portion of my receipts might be on the line as well.

It was even worse than I thought.

I read the letters a second time and then jammed them back into their envelopes. What was I going to do?

Nothing, right now. I just needed to deal with it in the morning.

I did a cursory and (in retrospect) pointless teeth brushing, changed into PJs, and with Winston snuggled in beside me, ate cookies and read a James Herriot book before turning off the light and trying to go to sleep.

Trying being the operative word.

And it wasn't just because I was listening for sounds of another break-in downstairs.

After all, how can you sleep when your ex-husband just turned up with a glamorous author; you've been told your business doesn't really belong to you; and the town council is trying to shut you down when you've only just opened?

I FINALLY GAVE up at around six a.m., having drifted into light off-and-on sleep. Mostly off. Light was leaking in through the curtains, brightening my bedroom; I got up and made myself a cup of coffee, then tossed on a pair of jeans and a T-shirt, leashed up Winston, and slipped on my tennis shoes. Maybe getting out for a walk would help dispel the cloud that had settled around me ever since I found out about my legal problems.

The air was cool and crisp and kissed with salt as I opened the door, the morning sun bright and full of promise. I took a sip of coffee from my thermal mug and locked the door behind me, feeling my spirits rise already.

I took Winston first up Cottage Street to Main Street, watching a few shop owners sweeping their front porches and getting ready for the day; the smell of bacon wafted to my nose, and the nasturtiums and lobelia in their planters glowed like jewels in the sunshine. The sky was blue and clear, and the sea breeze played with my hair as I walked past the ice cream store, and then the coffee shop where Denise had told me she was manager—it was pretty much the only thing open at this time of day, and seemed to be doing a brisk business. I glanced inside, but didn't see her; since I already had coffee, I walked on. From the card Nicholas had given me I remembered his address as being on Tourmaline Street; I took a detour off Main Street past the post office to the small, white-timbered house bearing the sign "Waters and Powers, Attorneys at Law." I hoped my mother was right and he'd have some ideas for getting me out of any legal entanglements.

On the way back to the bookstore, I passed the sand bar and cut down to the beach, listening to the lap of the waves against the rocks and shells as I searched for sea glass

A gull cried ahead of me. I looked up; somebody had left a pile of clothing on the beach, and the rising tide was starting to tug at it. I walked toward it, planning to pull it further up on the beach so I could come back down with a trash bag later, when I realized with a shock there was a hand bobbing up and down with the waves.

Winston began to growl, straining at the leash.

"Sssh," I said, and shortened the leash as I approached the body, hoping whoever it was might still be alive.

He wasn't.

And now I knew where my missing flatiron had gone.

It was embedded in his skull.

7

"Oh, no," I breathed, recognizing Cal Parker.

It was hard to believe that the same man who had almost yanked my arm out of the socket last night, very much alive, was now dead in the surf behind my store.

I reached for my phone and called 911, trying to quell a wave of nausea as I reported what I found. I couldn't stop looking at his pale face, eyes now open and unseeing, the water playing with his dark hair. A crab came and investigated his hand while I gave details to the dispatcher; I shooed it away.

I hung up the phone and hugged myself, still looking at the body. He was wearing the same clothes I'd seen him in last night—khakis and a blue-plaid shirt, with a navy windbreaker.

I examined him further, looking for anything else that might point to the identity of his murderer. Because it was definitely murder. You don't read about people committing suicide by beaning themselves in the head with a flatiron.

There was nothing obvious, although I found myself wondering where his phone was. Then, as the water shifted his jacket, I spotted what looked like a phone sticking out of the back pocket of his pants.

Still holding Winston on a short leash, I used Cal's jacket to pull the phone out. It was still functional; when I hit the button, some text messages popped up. One, from an anonymous number, at just before midnight. "Don't back out. We can fix the chatter. I've got it in the bag; I promise it'll work." And then, a few minutes later: "Please... just let's meet like we talked about." A third one from a DeeDee saying, "I'm so sorry we quarreled. I love you. I shouldn't have said anything." And a last one, at 1:32 a.m., again from DeeDee, saying, "Where are you? I'm worried. Please call."

I tucked the phone back into his pocket and stepped away from the body, looking at the flatiron. Someone must have taken it from the bookstore yesterday.

Had it happened during the signing?

And if so, who had taken it?

Since it seemed like half the town had been at the bookstore, it was going to be hard to narrow down.

Unless someone had nabbed it before the grand opening.

As I tried to remember when last I had seen it, a siren sounded from up near the store. I turned around and looked up as two paramedics jogged down to the beach carrying a stretcher.

I just hoped they'd also called the coroner.

THE POLICE SHOWED up not long after the paramedics, and within minutes, the beach was turned into a crime scene.

"You found the body?" a detective with brown, bobbed hair, a sharp chin and eyes that seemed to miss nothing asked me, a pad and pen at the ready. Her nametag identified her as R. Decker.

"I did, right before I called 911," I informed her.

She asked my name, jotted it down, then asked, "Did you know the victim?"

I nodded. "I met him at the grand opening last night. I spoke with him briefly."

"The grand opening? You mean the bookstore?" she asked, tilting her head toward Seaside Cottage Books.

"Yes. I'm the new owner."

"Huh." She wrote that down, then asked, "What did you talk to him about?"

"He... well, told me that I needed permits for the renovations I'd done, and that I needed to get the place inspected and approved within two weeks."

"That sounds kind of threatening."

I shrugged. "He suggested that maybe we could make a deal."

"Make a deal? How do you mean, exactly?"

"I don't know," I said.

"Did you meet him to talk about it?"

"No," I said. "I closed up and went upstairs for the rest of the night. Other than taking Winston out for a quick walk."

"When was that?"

"I'd say nine or so? I didn't leave after that."

She took down a note.

"And the object that was used in the attack," she said. "Had you seen that before?"

"I had, I believe."

"Where?"

"It functioned as a doorstop on the first floor of the bookshop." I shrugged. "But half the town was there yesterday. Any number of people could have taken it."

"When did you last see it?"

"I remember seeing it yesterday afternoon."

"Before the opening."

I nodded.

"But during the opening?"

"To be honest, I wasn't looking," I said. As I spoke, someone began photographing the body.

"Anyone else you know of who might have wished Cal Parker harm?" the detective asked, taking notes as she spoke.

I shook my head. "Like I said, I only met him yesterday."

"Not an auspicious meeting, though," she said. "What time did he leave the store?"

"I'm not sure. We closed at nine, but the last time I saw him must have been around eight."

"And did you see him afterwards?"

I shook my head. "No."

"May I ask your whereabouts last night?"

"Like I said, I finished cleaning up the place, then went up to my apartment and went to bed."

"Your apartment is above the shop?"

"Yes."

"Can anyone else vouch for your whereabouts?"

I looked down at Winston, who had moved close to my leg, as if he knew I was under threat. He cocked his fluffy white head at me. "Only Winston," I said.

"Winston's your dog?"

I nodded.

"Do you have anything in writing regarding these permits?"

"I have a letter from the Board of Selectmen," I said, "but I don't see what this has to do with what happened to Cal Parker."

All she said was, "Can I get a copy of that?"

"Of course," I said. "I'll make one today and get it to you."

"Actually, I'll have the original, if you don't mind."

I hesitated. I suspected she needed a warrant to go and get it, but I didn't want to look as if I wasn't cooperating. "No problem," I said, "I just need to make a copy of it. I need to talk to an attorney and find out what my options are, and I'd like to have all the paperwork in order."

"It seems to me that with Cal out of the way, maybe you won't have as much difficulty keeping the business going?"

"Cal wasn't the one who claimed to own half the store," I pointed out. "All he wanted to do was talk to me about permits, I think."

"Right," she said, writing that down. "Who did you buy the place from? Loretta Satterthwaite?"

"Yes," I confirmed. "It's her sister, Agatha, who is claiming she still owns half the property. At least according to Scooter."

"Did it seem to you that Agatha was driving the effort to reclaim the property? Or someone else?"

"I don't know," I said. "I just know that Scooter and Cal both seemed to know what was going on."

She touched the cap of the pen to her cheek and gave me a thoughtful look. "You don't have plans to leave town anytime soon, do you?"

"No," I said. "I just moved here the day before yesterday."

"Good," she said. "I think that's all for now, but I'll be wanting to talk to you again—and if you wouldn't mind being fingerprinted?"

"Of course," I said. "Although if the thing that killed Cal was from my shop, you're going to find my fingerprints on it. I know I've moved it more than once since I bought the shop."

"Even so," she said. "Why don't you go get that paper-work, and I'll have someone take your prints."

"Got it," I said, and with Winston at my heels, I turned away from the detective and the body on the beach, hoping that my stay in Snug Harbor wouldn't involve time behind bars.

*W*hen ten o'clock rolled around and I turned the sign at the front of the store to "Open," I was on my third cup of coffee, but the caffeine didn't seem to be helping much. After my interrogation, I'd showed the papers to the detective and had my fingerprints taken; despite multiple scrubbings, I couldn't get the ink off my fingers, which meant every time I looked down at my hands, I was reminded of what had happened—and of the fact that I was now a suspect in a murder case.

Since the flatiron was gone, I substituted an owl bookend I had brought from Boston, and tried to distract myself by watering the geraniums on the front porch and putting out some of the new stock that was still in boxes in the storage closet.

I really wanted to go upstairs and start putting my apartment to rights—I was feeling very out-of-sorts and discombobulated—but Bethany wasn't coming in till the afternoon, and someone had to woman the store.

Traffic picked up about twenty minutes after I opened. Unfortunately, it consisted mostly of locals, who spent a brief ten minutes perusing the shelves before shuffling over to find me and start asking questions.

"I heard you found Cal Parker down on the beach this morning. Nasty business. He was murdered?" asked one.

"Is it true he was going to close down the shop?" asked another.

"What are you going to do when you have to close the business?" was another question.

One thing you could say about small towns: news traveled fast.

By the time Denise popped in at eleven, I'd answered about fifty questions, but only sold one field guide to Maine wildflowers, two Ellery Adams mysteries, and a King James Bible. I'd given each customer one of the few leftover cookies from last night's shindig, fulfilling my " cookie with every purchase" promise, but I'd need to get back in the kitchen soon if I wanted to continue to make good on my offer.

"I heard what happened!" Denise announced, breathless, as she burst through the shop door. "Are you okay?"

"I think I'm still a little in shock," I told her, then held up my hands. "They printed me. I think I might be a suspect."

"A suspect? Why? You didn't even meet him until yesterday; that makes no sense at all."

"I'm afraid there's more to it than that," I said, and told her about the issue with the permits and the deed to the store.

"That slime ball," she said. "I've always wondered if he's not in cahoots with Scooter; he was probably going to get a kickback if you lost the property. I know Scooter was harassing Loretta about selling to him. I'm so sorry that happened to you."

"Thanks," I said.

She took a deep breath. "On a brighter note, I can't believe you're back in town!" she said, her face breaking into a familiar smile. "And I had no idea it was you buying the bookstore! This was always your favorite place as a kid; it's perfect for you!"

"Or sort of buying the shop, as it turns out."

She waved my objection away. "I'm sure it will all get worked out. Agatha can't possibly have a claim on the property."

"I wish it weren't so, but I think she may. Loretta and I did a really simple real estate transaction, and I don't think we did a title search," I told her.

"Oof," she said, wincing a little.

"Yeah. I'm hoping Nicholas can help me figure it out; I can't afford an attorney, but I thought maybe if I took him to lunch he could give me a cursory professional opinion."

"For old time's sake, you mean?" she said with a half-smile. "He's still pretty cute, you know."

"I did notice," I confirmed.

"And single."

"He mentioned that," I said. "But it's too soon for me to think about dating. I'm not ready to jump back into something else just yet, you know?"

She shrugged. "A few dates won't hurt. Help shake off the cobwebs. After all, your ex showed up in tow last night."

I groaned. "Don't remind me."

"With his girlfriend. The author. Did you know they were together?"

"I had no idea," I said. "But apparently, he's told her everything he knows about me, including my favorite foods. It's a little disconcerting."

"I'll bet," she said, brown eyes dancing. Except for her hair color, she hadn't changed much. She still had the same engaging smile, the same slight build, and the kind of energy that always made me think of Tigger.

"But enough about me," I said. "Didn't you say you were bringing scones or something?"

"And coffee," she said, holding up a carton with two paper cups and a pastry bag. "Where should we sit?"

"There's no one in the store, so let's go out to the porch."

"Sounds like a plan," she said, and I followed her back out the door to the front of the store, taking a deep breath and wondering once again at the difference between the diesel-scented air of Boston and Snug Harbor's salty, pine-tinged breezes.

"I do love it here," I said as she handed me a cup and I sat down on one of the rockers.

"Well, then, we just have to make sure you stay," she said. "Last night's receipts must have been good."

"They were," I said. "But tell me about you."

"Oh, not much to tell," she said, pulling two enormous blueberry muffins out of the bag and handing one to me. As she spoke, I took a big bite, and just about swooned. Sweet, moist blueberries, soft, slightly tangy muffin, and crystal-lized sugar that added a sweet blast of crunch.

"These are amazing," I told her.

"You think?" She smiled. "It's my recipe; I've been working on it for years. We just started selling them."

"I'll take all of them," I said, and she laughed. "But I didn't mean to interrupt; tell me more."

She took a big bite of muffin herself first, and when she'd swallowed, she took a swig of coffee and gave me the short version. "I went to school for a couple of years, got an English degree. Spent some time in New York City and L.A., trying out some corporate jobs, but I missed Snug Harbor, so I came home. I manage the coffee shop now, but my dream is to own a shop of my own."

"It was the same way for me in Boston," I said. "Although I hadn't realized I wanted to own my own shop until Ellie— my manager—suggested I look into Seaside Cottage Books. She couldn't make it to the opening, but she's going to come up this week on her day off."

"I can't wait to meet her," Denise said. "What made you decide to go for it?"

"Ellie offered me an assistant manager position in Boston, but there was no way I could afford rent with the salary. And Loretta and I came up with something I could manage—barely— so I went for it."

"Good for you," she said. "You're an inspiration. How are you with the whole... divorce thing?" she asked, compassion in her eyes. "It must have been hard seeing your ex with someone else so soon."

"It's fresh," I admitted. "It's still sinking in."

"I'm sure the grief will still come, at the most unexpected moments. But I know it will get better." She reached out to grasp my hand as the tears rose to my eyes. We hadn't seen each other in years, but despite everything that had happened in the interim decades, it was as if that day on the playground had been just a few days ago.

"Thanks," I said in a husky voice, and swiped at my eyes. "Whatever happened to Donny Knee, anyway? Do you know?"

"He still lives with his parents and works down at the library," she said. "He's part of the town; we all look out for him."

"Life as it should be," I said. As I spoke, a woman with a purposeful stride and an unpleasant set to her mouth stopped at the end of the walkway and marched up the front walk.

"Is that Agatha Satterthwaite?" Denise asked under her breath.

"I have no idea," I said. "I've never met her."

"It is," she confirmed as the woman came closer. "Gird your loins. She looks like she's spoiling for a fight."

The woman stopped a few yards from the store. Her eyes swept over it with a proprietary air, then came to rest first on Denise, and then me. As I sipped my coffee, she marched up to the porch and put her hands on her hips. "You're Maxine Sayers," she announced. She wore boots, a long black skirt, and a gray blouse that buttoned all the way up to her chin and was covered with a lint-specked cardigan; something about her reminded me of a visitor from the late 1800s.

"I'm Max," I confirmed.

"I came by three times this week and you weren't here."

"Bethany mentioned someone had come by," I said. "Can I get you a coffee, or a cookie, or something? I'm afraid we don't have enough muffins..."

"No," she said shortly. "I'm not here to be buttered up. You're on my property."

"I know about your, uh, claims," I said. "I'm sure we'll be able to clear everything up."

"You'll clear it up when you pay me my share," she sniffed. "My sister tried to put one over on both of us. Always did act like she was the only one in the family."

"Like I said, I'm sure we'll get it cleared up," I said. "In the meantime, you're welcome to go in and browse if you like."

"Nope," she said. "Just wanted to make sure you knew what the situation was. If you don't come to the terms in the letter in thirty days, I'm taking you to court. By the way, I had an appraisal done."

"You did?"

"It's right here," she said. "I wanted to give it to you in person. You took advantage of my sister, and I plan to right the wrong." As she spoke, she fished a battered manila envelope out of the cloth grocery bag she had slung over her left shoulder. "Here," she said. "There's an appraisal in there and a bill for what you didn't pay."

The envelope felt heavy in my hand. "I'll take a look at it," I assured her.

"As I'm sure you know, you can refer any questions to my attorney, Scooter Dempsey," she said.

"I will. By the way, did you hear the news?" I asked.

"What news?"

"Cal Parker was murdered on the beach this morning," I said.

An expression that might have been surprise crossed her face, and then her jaw snapped shut and her face hardened. "What does that have to do with anything? You're trying to bilk me out of my inheritance."

"Bilk you out of your inheritance?"

"Our mother changed her will. She willed the property to both of us, not just Loretta," Agatha said. "Scooter found the second will."

"Found it where?"

"At her attorney's office," she said. "Well, missy," she said, shaking a finger at me, "you've got another thing coming if you think I'm going to roll over. I'll bet you killed that selectman, too, for trying to mess with your store."

"What? You're kidding me, right?" I asked in disbelief.

She raised her chin. "I'm going to the police right now to tell them what you did."

"I already talked to the police," I said. "I don't think you can tell them anything they don't already know."

"They don't know you're a murderer," she spat, "or you wouldn't be drinking coffee on my porch, looking pleased as punch." With that, she whirled around, her skirt flaring out and exposing narrow, pale calves that looked like they'd never seen the sun.

Denise and I watched her hurry down the walk and take a sharp left, moving with new purpose.

"The police station's that way," Denise observed, taking another sip of her coffee.

"I gathered," I said, looking down at the envelope that lay heavy in my lap. "Do I open this?"

"I always prefer to face bad news head on, but it's up to you."

I took another bite of muffin to give me courage and pinched open the brass clip on the back. When I tipped the envelope over, a stack of papers slid into my lap with a *thunk*. On the top was a letter from Agatha claiming that the value of her share of the property was thrice what I'd paid for Seaside Cottage Books, and that she was entitled to that amount.

"There's no way," I said as I looked at the cover letter.

"What?"

"She wants three times the money I paid for the place," I said. "And after all the work I put into it..."

"If she's working with Scooter, you know she's not planning on moving in."

"They want to raze it, don't they?"

She nodded. "No doubt he wants to put in some big mixed-use retail place so he can make bank. I think he recently picked up a few more waterfront properties. It's all about money for him." She took a sip of her coffee.

"He's successful?" I asked.

"Oh, yes," she said. "Usually through loopholes and a

predatory instinct, from what I hear. Buying distressed properties, putting the pressure on people to sell, finding out-of-
state and foreign investors... you know."

"So really adding to the sense of community," I said
dryly.

"Exactly. I'll bet he drummed up Agatha's claim and
convinced her to go after you. And hired the appraiser, too."

"There is a package from an appraiser in here. I should
probably look at it, shouldn't I?" I asked, poking at the stack
of paper like it was a dead fish.

"Probably," she said. "But you already know the price
they're asking for it."

I groaned and opened it up. Sure enough, they'd
appraised the property for hundreds of thousands more
than I'd paid for it. "They appraised it after I made the
improvements!" I said. "That's not fair!"

"That you can contest, I'm sure, but I don't think the
improvements are going to knock the price down by two-
thirds."

I looked through it and my heart sank. "She did give me
a deal on the property. I had no idea."

Denise sighed. "The council's been holding the line in
terms of development, particularly with properties owned
by out-of-town investors, but ever since Cal Parker bought
his way onto the council, the tide has turned."

"What do you mean?"

"He is—or was, rather—voting yes on things the old
council never would have approved. And a lot of people say
our old friend Scooter was lining his pockets."

"So I'm not the only one he's targeted?"

"Nope," she said, shaking her head. "Half the town
couldn't stand him."

"And the other half?"

"They were dumb enough to have believed his promise to cut taxes and make life here even more touristy. Some people like that idea, but most of us kind of like things as they've been, you know?"

"I know," I said. "It's a balance."

"Not anymore," she said. "Although with Cal Parker out of the way..."

I took a sip of coffee. "I think I'm Suspect Number One."

9

"I already told you that's ridiculous," Denise scoffed. "You never met him before yesterday."

"But he threatened my business." I looked at her. "And whoever did him in used the flatiron I repurposed as a doorstop."

"Wait. The murder weapon came from the shop?"

I nodded.

"But half the town was here last night!"

"I know. And I told them my prints are all over it."

"That must be why they printed you. To eliminate your prints."

"Then why did she ask me not to leave town?"

Denise winced. "Yeah. That is a problem."

She was about to say something else when a woman I didn't recognize trotted up the sidewalk and turned into the path leading to the bookstore, almost running up to the porch. She stopped when she saw us, the strings of her apron flapping in the breeze and her chest heaving.

"Is it true?" she asked, wild-eyed.

"Is what true?"

"Is Councilman Parker dead?"

"I'm afraid so," I said.

"Murdered?"

I nodded.

She swallowed, and something—fear?—crossed her face. "You found him, right?" she asked, addressing the question to me. "How did he die?" she asked, staring. Her eyes were bloodshot, and she was wringing her apron, a hand-stitched checked number that appeared to have seen a lot of use, in her hands.

"I don't know that I'm allowed to say," I told her, glancing at Denise.

"It was... violent?"

I hesitated, then nodded. She sucked in her breath.

"Were you close with him?" I asked.

"Close?" She blinked, then let out a hard sound that was something between a sob and a guffaw. "No. I rue the day he set foot in Snug Harbor." And with that, she turned around and headed back down the path, walking slowly this time, her shoulders drooping.

When she was out of earshot, I turned to Denise. "Who the heck was that?"

"Sylvia Berland," she informed me. "She and her husband own the Salty Dog Brew Pub."

"Why was she so upset about what happened to Cal Parker?"

Denise glanced at me. "I imagine she's afraid her husband Jared might be responsible."

"Why?"

"Cal's been going after all kinds of business owners, telling them they need extra permits, or they're not in compliance with town law... just being a pain in the neck. The Salty Dog has been in his crosshairs lately; he's saying the pub is too close to a school, even though it's a half mile down the road."

"What was in it for Cal?"

"I think he made 'deals' with businesses... they'd pay to be forgiven, if that makes sense."

"Graft, in other words. But aren't there other selectmen? Why was he so powerful?"

She took another bite of muffin. "There are five, but at least two of them seem to have been in Cal's back pocket."

"But he was just elected, so he's junior."

"There are a lot of theories about why that might be," she said. "He was a wealthy man. He had power. I'm guessing he dug up dirt on them and they were afraid he'd run smear campaigns and get them ousted."

"Mudslinging."

"His specialty," she said. "And rich as he was, he didn't seem to be averse to making more dollars, even at the expense of those who are just getting by."

"And he and Scooter were close, you say? No surprise there."

"I know. I wonder which one of them came up with the idea of setting Agatha on you?"

"What's Agatha's deal, anyway?"

"She's bitter... she and her parents had a falling-out years ago. Loretta took care of their mom during her last years. I don't know this for sure, but I heard their mom gave Agatha some of the money she had left, but left the store to Loretta."

"Why is Agatha contesting it, then? It sounds like it was a reasonably equitable settlement, right?"

"This is a valuable piece of property," Denise said. "I'm guessing once Agatha got wind of what Loretta sold it to you for—or, rather, when Scooter informed her that she'd sold it to you—she started looking for ways to get her piece of the pie."

"She has no reason to have wanted to kill Cal Parker, though. Me, on the other hand..."

"Oh, you're not the only suspect. Lots of dysfunctional families in Snug Harbor; Cal's brother is a prime suspect, too."

"His brother?"

"Josiah Parker. He's had it in for his brother for years."

"Well, that's something, I guess." I sighed. I'd thought Snug Harbor would be a refuge from the big, bad, scary world, but there are rotten eggs everywhere.

And unfortunately, I reflected, one of them had ended up cracked open right behind my shop.

DENISE HEADED out at around noon, just as lunch-break customers started drifting into the shop. If nothing else, I reflected as I fielded yet another question about the murder and sold a hardbound P.G. Wodehouse collection, the news was good for business.

"I heard you dated him a long time ago," one woman said.

"No," I said pleasantly. "I'd never met him before last night."

"Wasn't he going to kick you out of your store?" someone else asked as he walked over to the register with a copy of the Farmer's Almanac.

"Not exactly," I said, and then, to change the subject, "What kind of cookie would you like?"

Bethany turned up just after two, evidently the only resident of Snug Harbor unaware of what had happened behind Seaside Cottage Books. The early sun was slanting through the windows, making the polished wood floors glow; I'd opened the windows, and a cool breeze filtered through the shop, smelling of the sea.

"How are sales going today?" she asked as she breezed through the front door.

"Good," I said, "but did you hear what happened?"

"No," she said. "What's up?"

By the time I finished telling her, her face had gone from happy to sad to determined.

"There's no way we're going to let this shop go down," she announced with the optimism of youth. "And there's no way you killed Cal Parker." She glanced at me. "Not that I'd blame you if you did. In fact, it was kind of a public service."

"Still."

"I know, I know," she said.

"You know this town inside and out," I told her. "Sylvia Berland from the Salty Dog came by earlier; Denise thinks she's worried her husband Jared may be responsible. From what I hear, Cal was making life difficult for a lot of folks in Snug Harbor."

"You're not wrong," she said.

"We need to make a list of all the people he's ticked off."

"We could probably fill one of those blank books," she said, pointing to the display of journals I'd set up close to the register. "It's a testament to the power of money that he got elected, frankly."

"Well, then," I said, reaching for a pad of legal paper and a pen. "Let's get started. Who's first?"

Bethany grabbed a duster and began running it over the tops of the books on the shelves as she considered my question; there was still a good bit of dust from some of the renovations we'd done. "His ex-wife, of course," she led off with as she swept the duster over, perhaps appropriately, the romance section, going back to retrieve a feather that had fallen onto a buxom young lady's barely satin-clad bosom. I was looking forward to finding out who in Snug Harbor was a romance devotee; you could find out a lot about a person based on the books they chose.

"What do you know about his ex-wife, Gretchen?" I asked, watching as she moved on to the science fiction and fantasy section.

"She lives just outside of town; they divorced two years ago when she found him with one of the administrative assistants in the copy room. Unfortunately, he'd talked her into signing a pre-nup, so she's been working as a waitress at the Chart House and cursing his name ever since."

"She was here yesterday, wasn't she?" I asked. "I talked to her... she told me her ex was in cahoots with Scooter."

Bethany nodded. "Hair in a French twist, wore a pink dress, shot daggers out of her eyes at her ex for the five minutes they were in the store together."

"So she stays on the list," I said, circling her name. "Who else?"

"Well, there's the councilwoman he unseated, of course."

"I met her last night, too," I said. "Meryl Ferguson."

"That's the one," she said. "If looks could kill, Cal would have been dead at least twice over before he left the shop."

"I got the impression she had an ax to grind, to say the least. So that's two possibilities," I said, feeling slightly brighter. "He wasn't the most popular guy in town, was he?"

"No," she said.

"What else do you know about him?"

"I think he's got a string of ex-girlfriends, but nobody I know personally. Oh... and he's also been causing trouble for the Chinese restaurant on the corner of Cottage and

Garden Streets. They were trying to get a liquor license, and he's taken that opportunity to find all kinds of violations."

"Why was he going after them?"

"Well, rumor has it one of his companies bought two other buildings on that block, and they've got a five-year lease they're only two years into, from what I hear."

"So if they went out..."

"He would have been able to upgrade the space and rent it out for more money. Or go high and do condos."

"Very quaint," I said dryly. "Isn't that a conflict of interest, though?"

"Who was going to go after him?" she asked. "The restaurant is in violation of some of the more archaic codes, evidently, and there's no proof that his plans were to turn the whole block into something profitable for him."

"That's the pits," I said, thinking again that it was hard to believe such language would come from a young woman almost half my age. She spoke like an English professor. In fact, she spoke more eloquently and precisely than many English professors I'd met.

"Exactly," she said.

"Why was he after the bar, then? Is that to make money?"

"Oh, no," she said. "He thought his ex-wife cheated on him with Jared."

"So he was trying to shut him down?"

"That's the word on the street," she said. Bethany grinned at me. "All kinds of intrigue in town, isn't there?"

"On the plus side, at least I'm not the only suspect in Snug Harbor."

"No," she said. "But he was found dead behind your store. And you did agree to talk to him later."

"And it was my doorstop embedded in his head."

She shrugged. "There is that."

I sighed. "Does he have any family?"

"His parents passed some time back; he picked up their business. He has a brother, though."

"Is he involved with the business, too?"

"Nope. He never went to college; he just wanted to be a fisherman."

"Not even a stake?"

"From what I hear, the whole business went to Cal."

"Huh," I said, enjoying the breeze filtering through the windows as I rearranged the Maine section. "Money seems to be a bit of a problem in families. Maybe it's a good thing I don't have an inheritance coming my way."

"That's one way to look at it," she said. "I can tell you, there's no love lost there. Josiah campaigned against his brother in the election."

"Wow. Really?"

"Spent weeks handing out leaflets talking about what a selfish jerk his brother was. It didn't work, of course." She shook her head. "I guess blood isn't always thicker than water."

"No kidding," I said. As I turned a book on the history of Snug Harbor face out, on a whim, I took it down and flipped through it, glancing at the pictures of the town before electricity and cars. I recognized several of the big cottages down on the shore, the trees that were now enormous mere saplings.

"Who lives in these now?" I asked, showing them to Bethany.

"Cal Parker does... or did, anyway... for starters," she said. "Although a lot of them have been turned into inns. If you can find the Windswept house, that's his."

I flipped through until I found the page. "This one?" I asked, pointing to a picture of a massive, gorgeous Tudor-style house with a sprawling lawn.

"That's the one," she said. "Has a gorgeous view of the harbor and about nine thousand bedrooms."

"Only nine thousand?" I asked, grinning. "And his brother lives where?"

"In a shack not too far from the gas station."

"Wow," I said, looking at the enormous home in the picture. Had Cal Parker's parents really disowned one son in favor of the other? If so, why? I wondered.

And could that have something to do with why Cal died?

"So Cal is really invested in Snug Harbor."

"He is."

"What I don't get is, if he had a successful business, why would he want to be a selectman?"

"Men like Cal Parker are all about power," she told me, her young face solemn. As she spoke she ran her duster over the windowsill, which was decorated with Mason jars of blue and green sea glass that glowed in the sunlight. "He wants to put his stamp on Snug Harbor. I guess he figures the best way to do that is to control the reins of government."

"That makes sense, I suppose."

"Honestly? I think selectman was just his first step. He poured more money into his campaign than Snug Harbor has ever seen."

"It worked, apparently," I said. I put my hand on the wall; it had likely stood here for more than a hundred years. "With him gone, though, maybe they'll lay off on the code stuff?"

"Maybe," she said. "We've got to vote in a replacement, so at least we've got some time."

"Do you really think Scooter Dempsey wants to raze this place and put something huge and ugly here?"

"I guarantee it," she said, pointing her duster at me. "He

and Cal Parker were thick as thieves. They've partnered on multiple ventures."

"Great," I said, with that sick feeling again. If Agatha was right, and there was in fact a second will, it looked like divorce might not be the worst thing I had to deal with that year.

*a*t six, I decided to leave Bethany, who was doing her history homework behind the register, in charge. I retrieved Winston from his fluffy bed clipped a leash to his collar, and grabbed my travel mug with the last remains of coffee in it.

"We're going to go for a walk before it gets dark and maybe grab something to eat," I told Bethany. "Do you need me to pick anything up for you?"

"I'm good," she said. "Enjoy yourself; you could use a break after today."

"Call me if you need me, okay?" It was still bright outside, but the summer sun was dipping down toward the hills inland, giving everything a magical golden glow.

I couldn't bear going down to the beach at the moment —at least not behind the house—so I headed out to the sidewalk in front of the shop, heading down toward the town pier and Windswept, the house Cal lived in until his death.

I strolled past summer vacationers, families wearing windbreakers against the cooling air and licking ice cream cones as they ambled in and out of the souvenir shops. A whiff of balsam reached my nose as I passed Snug Harbor Gifts, which had always been my favorite store for locally made souvenirs, including balsam fir sachets in bright prints that I planned to load up on and tuck into my dresser drawers... once I had time, that was. And money. The *Abigail Todd* was about to head out for its sunset sail, the vacationgoers filing up the gangway to the four-masted sailing ship. Many of them, I noticed, were still in short sleeves and shorts; I hoped they had warmer gear in their purses and backpacks, or they might find their cruise a little chilly.

The two cannons that had been placed on a grassy knoll in earlier, more dangerous times to protect the harbor were now jungle gyms and photo op locations for families; I could hear the "orders" of two girls pretending to aim for the *Abigail Todd* as I walked past them toward the shoreline path, which was just above the beach and backed the massive "cottages" I'd seen pictured in the book of Snug Harbor's history.

The bustle of town was soon left behind, and the beauty of the Gulf of Maine stretched out below me as I stepped onto the well-kept path. Beach roses grew in tufts along the path, their winey scent perfuming the salt air, and below me, folks clambered over the occasional boulder or strolled down by the water's edge, searching for treasures left by the tide.

My attention, though, was not on the sea glass gems the tide washed up, but the massive homes perched above the shore path. Although many of them had burned in a fire almost a hundred years ago, and several more had been torn down over the years, several still stood in commanding positions over the Shore Path. I passed an enormous red brick compound, followed by a beautiful shingle-style home that reminded me of Seaside Cottage Books, only on an extremely powerful dose of steroids, and then reached Windswept, the large Tudor home owned by the late Cal Parker. Whereas the other homes had landscaping that allowed at least a peek into the grounds, Windswept was hidden by a fence and a large hedge to keep the hoi polloi from peeking in on the councilman's private life. I slowed my gait as I came to the house, pausing at the wooden gate and stepping back a bit, trying to glimpse the house. All I could see, though, was the slate roof and the mullioned windows of the top floor. Even if I hadn't seen pictures in the book at the store, it was obvious that the house was huge; it had enough rooms to house an entire village, not just one person. I caught a whiff of fresh-cut grass mingling with the scent of roses and salt air as I cased the hedge, stooping over and trying to look through the dense leaves without looking like a peeping Tom. Thank goodness for Winston, who was moving slowly beside me, sniffing the edge of the path intently, looking for the perfect place to do his business.

As I squinted and tried to see through the leaves, I heard voices from the other side of the greenery.

The first was a man's. "Do you really think the woman who owned the bookstore did him in?"

"No," replied a woman. "I'll bet whoever did it was much closer to home. A lot more people with a lot more reason to bash in his skull than some outsider who just moved to town."

"Maybe," the man said, but he didn't sound convinced. "What do you think will happen now?"

"I don't know," the woman said ominously, "but I'm going to start looking for another job. I hear Saltaire is looking for maid staff." I looked down at Winston, who had found just the place to water the hedge and was now pulling at the leash, hoping for a chance to chase a sea gull who had landed not far up the path. I shook my head at him and willed him not to bark, but I could already hear the growl starting in his chest. "Shhh!" I whispered, straining to hear the voices beyond the hedge.

"Do you think Josiah killed him?" the man suggested.

"Could be. No love lost between those two."

"I'm glad he wasn't my brother."

"Me too. You'd think he'd have been nicer to family, wouldn't you? Anyway, it could be Josiah, but I wouldn't rule the girlfriend out. They had a big argument about getting hitched the other night." I perked up my ears even more.

"He wasn't going for it?" the man asked.

"Nope. She told him to go to hell, and good for her. I was dusting the hallway outside the master bedroom when they got into it—I'd just brought them some of that French champagne he likes—so I heard everything. She said if he didn't put a ring on it after all this time, she was going to leave and tell everyone about what he was doing down on Cottage Street."

"What was he doing? What was she talking about, do you think?"

"I don't know, but he didn't like it."

"I'll bet. Did he go after her?" The voices were moving away; I hurried up the shore path further, straining to hear.

"I don't know if he laid a hand on her, but I'll tell you, the tone of his voice made my hair curl. If it wasn't already curly, that is. He said she should remember who she was talking to, and what she had to lose. Real cold like."

"That sounds bad."

"It was. She shut up in a hurry, especially when he said something about a video."

"He always covered his tracks. You don't cross Mr. Parker," the man said in a knowing voice.

"Well, someone did," the woman pointed out. "And I kind of hope they get away with it." Before I could hear more, Winston yanked on the leash and started barking in full cry at the sea gull, who just looked at him placidly. As I scooped him up, the voices drifted away, back toward the house. I bent down and tried to peek through the hedge, curious to identify the speakers, but the dark leaves were too dense; I couldn't see who it was.

Who was the woman they were talking about? I wondered as I put Winston down and let him lead me toward the sea gull, who lazily took wing when Winston was three feet away, leaving him disappointed as always.

I watched the sea gull soaring above, wishing I had its view of Windswept. What exactly had the mystery woman had on Cal Parker?

And had whatever he had on her been enough to make her bash his brains out on the beach behind my shop?

11

J finished walking the shoreline trail, thinking about the conversation I'd heard and checking my Fitbit to see my progress—I had gotten it not long ago and was trying hard to get my steps in and eliminate some of the excess fluffiness that had collected around my waist since the divorce. I'd been so anxious leading up to the mediation that I practically stopped eating, allowing me, for a brief six weeks, to fit into clothes I hadn't worn since my twenties. As soon as things were resolved, however, my body had clamored for all the fudgy goodness it hadn't wanted the previous six months. Before long, between my caramel latte addiction and my brownie-baking habit, all of the pounds that had melted away prior to the big day had returned. And some of them brought friends.

I followed one of the side streets back into town, trying to get a glimpse of Windswept from the front. The fence along the back turned into a wall in the front, though; even the gate for entering cars was made of solid wood, and unless I wanted to stop and peer through the slats, there was no way to see in. But as I walked by, there was a whirring noise, and the gate slid open behind me.

As I watched, a low, sleek, forest-green Jaguar purred out of the gate, a woman with black hair and enormous, expensive-looking sunglasses at the wheel. Her diamond pendant earring twinkled in the sun as she turned left, intent on her destination, not noticing me at all.

I took the opportunity to backtrack a few steps and peek into the compound as the gate shut. I could see the enormous Tudor facade, set off by a lawn that was beautifully landscaped with roses and trailing ivy, and two cars. One, right in front of the house, was a gorgeous, wood-sided antique car. The other, an ancient Honda whose body was half rust, squatted in a gravel drive that led to what looked like a carriage house half-tucked behind the mansion, and probably close to the servant's entrance. I thought I saw a glimpse of a woman with dark hair in one of the upstairs windows before the gates nicked shut.

I looked down at Winston, who was impatient with my stops and starts and anxious to move on and check out more of the olfactory landscape. "Sorry, buddy," I murmured, and we walked on toward town, following the direction the woman had gone.

As Winston investigated the curb lining the road, I found myself wondering about the driver of the sleek, expensive car. Was she the woman who had threatened Cal the night before? If not, why was she at the house? I'd have to ask Bethany and Denise if they knew who she was... or who Cal had been seeing. One of them, I couldn't remember who, had said he had dated multiple people. Had one of his girlfriends found out about another?

There was one thing I could say for Cal Parker: he

certainly seemed to have had a lot of people angry at him before he died.

I walked home slowly, passing several cute and sleepy houses before I was back in Snug Harbor proper, I relished the colorful shop windows and the gorgeous planters, which were overflowing with jewel-like orange and red nasturtiums, white and crimson geraniums, and vivid purple lobelia. As Winston sniffed at a particularly lovely container garden in a whiskey barrel, I made a mental note to add some plantings to the barrels of geraniums at the front of the shop; a few more pops of color would make the already adorable shingle-style building even more enchanting.

As I passed the Snug Harbor Suncatchers store, entranced by the brilliant stained-glass creations that twirled in the morning breeze, I caught a glimpse of myself in the empty store window across the street and winced. I hadn't looked in the mirror before I left the store; I'd scrunched my hair up in a ponytail when I was standing behind the register, and now a big chunk was standing up in a lump on the left side of my head. Thank goodness I hadn't seen anyone I knew yet... not that I knew that many people in Snug Harbor these days anyway. But I had just reached up to fix that hair lump when around the corner appeared Nicholas, who was staring down at his phone and carrying a paper cup of coffee with Sea Beans' logo.

Or had been, until he ran into me.

AS WE COLLIDED, his coffee cup jolted out of his hand, covering both of us in warm, milky latte.

"Oh my gosh... I'm so sorry!" I said, my hand still in my

lumpy hair and my T-shirt now covered in coffee, which thankfully was no longer piping hot.

Nicholas was also covered in coffee, but unlike me, he was wearing nicer clothes—khakis and a green button-down shirt, both of which were now liberally splotched. To my relief, he grinned at me, then bent to retrieve my travel mug.

"Why are you sorry? We both ran into each other."

"I just wasn't paying attention," I said, about to tell him I was checking myself out in the store window across the street, then catching myself just in time. Something about the way he looked at me made my face heat up. I suddenly realized I still had an enormous hair lump on the top of my head. I yanked the rubber band out of my hair and attempted to fluff it nonchalantly, wishing I'd taken five minutes to at least glance at myself in the mirror before heading out the door.

"Me neither," he said. "I just got a text from a client, and should have been watching where I was going instead of attempting to type with my thumbs. I'm just thankful you weren't a Suburban."

I laughed. Speaking of texts, I hadn't heard from my girls in a while, and I had some questions to ask them. Like, about why nobody had mentioned my ex was dating K. T. Anderson, glamorous bestselling author extraordinaire. Although it wasn't a fair question; that really was his responsibility to share, not theirs, now that I thought of it.

"I heard you had a bit of a surprise this morning," he said. "I'm sorry you were the one who had to find him."

"Cal Parker? Yeah. It was a bit of a shock," I admitted.

"You and your canine companion found him on your morning walk? That's what the Snug Harbor grapevine is saying. Which isn't entirely to be trusted, although at least they didn't have you toting along a wagon filled with monkeys."

"A wagon full of monkeys?"

"Sometimes a bit of embellishment happens as news travels," he said. "I also heard that the cops printed you."

I held up my still stained fingertips. "They did," I said.

"Not the best welcome back to town, is it?"

"No," I said. "And you don't know the half of it." I told him about Agatha Satterthwaite's claim.

He sighed. "That's got Scooter written all over it."

"Speaking of Scooter..." I blushed, thinking of the rumors he had spread about me all those years ago.

"Ancient history," Nicholas said shortly, before I had a chance to say another word, and gave me a tight smile. "Did you do a title search when you bought the property?"

"Uh, no," I said sheepishly. "Loretta and I kind of managed it as a personal transaction, to cut agent commission costs."

He grimaced. "That's not good news."

My heart sank. "Is there anything I can do? My understanding is that she owned the place outright, or I never would have bought it."

"She signed a quitclaim deed?"

I nodded.

"So you at least own half of it," he said. "Presuming the will split the property between them."

"That's good news, right?"

"It's not the worst-case scenario, anyway. But Agatha would still own the other half."

"Great," I said.

He looked down at his shirt and pants, and then glanced at his phone. "I hate to run, but I probably should head home and change; I've got a meeting in thirty minutes."

"Oh... I'm sorry to hold you up."

"No worries," he said, with the lopsided grin that had captured my heart back in eighth grade. "I'll see what I can dig up on your case," he added as he picked up his coffee cup and deposited it into a nearby trash can.

"I really appreciate it," I told him. "See you soon." I started back on my way with Winston.

"Oh, and Max?" he called after I'd moved on about ten steps.

"Yes?" I asked, whirling around.

"I'm glad you're back in town," he said, and my heart turned over in my chest.

BY THE TIME I got home, my heart rate had almost returned to normal, and as I opened the door to my still-boxed-up kitchen, I was caught between floating on cloud nine and falling into a pit of despair. It was a weird place to be.

I'd just finished changing out of my coffee-stained clothes and fixing my hair in the mirror (still a big lump, much to my embarrassment), when my cell phone burbled in the back pocket of the jeans I'd recently changed out of. I managed to pull it out of the pocket and answer it just before it went to voicemail. It was my daughter, Audrey.

12

"Mom?" she said, voice tentative.

"Hey, Audrey," I said. "How's the summer job treating you?"

"Fine," she said. She was interning at a local non-profit, I knew. "I talked to Dad last night," she said cautiously.

"Oh?" I asked.

"Yeah. He mentioned you two, uh, ran into each other at the store's grand opening."

"We did," I confirmed. There was a moment of silence.

"Sorry I didn't tell you," she finally blurted. "It's just... I didn't want to get in the middle of it, and it's so awkward, and I don't know what I think, and..."

My heart melted, and I sat down on the foot of my unmade air mattress, sinking almost all the way to the floor. I eyed my real mattress, which was propped up against the wall, and vowed to make at least some progress in my living space that evening. "It's okay, sweetheart. We're all finding our way through this. I understand how awkward it must be for you."

"You do? Really? It's just... I don't know what to do. I

mean, she's nice and all, and Dad seems happy—they're like high schoolers, oh my gosh, I shouldn't have just told you that—but it's so weird!"

My heart twisted a little, but I reassured her. "I get it," I told her. "It's weird for me, too. But we both love you so much, and I really am glad he's doing okay." Even if he was now going by Theodore.

"I just felt so bad meeting her and not telling you about it... I feel like such an awful daughter, and..."

"No." I stopped her mid-sentence. "You don't need to get involved in what happens between Dad and me. That's our job," I said.

"Really?"

"Really," I said. "And that goes for your sister, too."

"Thanks," she said, and I could hear the relief in her voice. "She's mad, but she really does love you; I think she'll come around."

"Thanks," I said. "Is everything going okay for her?"

"It is," she said. "She's just... adjusting. Is my puppy doing okay?" she asked, changing the subject.

"Winston is great," I said, looking down at his smiling face. "We just got back from a walk."

"I'll bet he loves all the new smells." She knew our little dog well. "I miss him so much. How did the opening go?"

"Fine," I said.

"What's wrong?" she asked.

"What? Nothing."

"I know better than that. Spill it. Is it what's going on with Dad?"

"No," I said, truthfully. "It's just some bureaucratic red tape, is all."

"Bureaucratic red tape?"

"I'm sure I'll get it worked out."

"Whatever it is, it sounds bad. Are you sure you're okay?"

"It'll be fine," I said lightly, even though I wasn't sure it would be fine at all. But Audrey had enough on her plate right now; between coping with our divorce, figuring out how to be a college student and holding down her first job, she didn't need to be pulled into my drama. Although if they cuffed me and threw me in jail for murder, she might not have a choice.

Stop being dramatic, I chided myself; from what I knew of Cal, stronger suspects were thick on the ground. I'd only just met the man yesterday. I'd only been angry at him for 12 hours before I found him dead. Plenty of other people had evidently been mad at him for years.

Audrey spent the next ten minutes telling me about her job, and the weekend trip she was planning with friends, and I felt my heart swell with love and pride. She'd been a shy but super-bright girl, and I loved watching her not just come into her own in school, but finally learn to make and nurture friendships. "It sounds like things are going great, Audrey."

"They are. Oh, and I met someone," she added, off-handedly. That was a first; she hadn't had any apparent interest in dating all through high school, and I'd never heard her mention anyone since starting college.

"Really?" I asked. Love appeared to be in the air for everyone but me, I thought. Then the image of Nicholas' lopsided smile floated into my thoughts. I banished it. "Who is he?" I asked, returning my focus to my daughter.

"His name is Blake," she said. "He's pre-med. We met at a coffee shop, and he's taken me out to dinner three times. I think you'll like him."

"I'm sure I will," I said. "I'd love to meet him when you're ready."

"Of course," she said. "Hey... I've got to go, but thanks for talking. I love you. And I hope you get whatever it is worked out."

"I love you too, Pumpkin," I said, and hung up with a smile on my face. I might not have gotten my marriage right. I might not have gotten the purchase of Seaside Cottage Books right. But my kids were all right, and that meant more to me than anything.

BY THE TIME Winston and I made it down to open the bookstore the next morning, I'd deflated and folded up the air mattress, maneuvered my mattress onto my bedroom floor, made it up with fresh sheets, and emptied two boxes of kitchen stuff. It wasn't much, but it was a start.

Downstairs, as Winston curled up in his bed, I turned the shop sign to OPEN and picked up the stack of papers that had been delivered to the front porch that morning. As I set the string-tied bundle on the counter, the above-the-fold headline caught my eye: LOCAL SELECTMAN FOUND DEAD: FOUL PLAY SUSPECTED. Below it was a picture of the beach behind the bookstore, the peaceful scene marred by yellow crime scene tape and men and women in uniform. No sign of the body in the picture, thankfully.

I reread the headline and shook my head. Suspected? I thought as I pulled the top paper out from the bundle and spread it on the desk. How else did someone end up with a flatiron embedded in the back of his head if not foul play?

I scanned the article, dismayed to find my name in the second paragraph. "He was discovered by Maxine Sayers, new owner of Seaside Cottage Books. Parker had recently threatened to issue the business owner a citation for operating improperly."

I swallowed the lump that had formed in my throat. Had the journalist who wrote the article just drawn a link between Cal Parker's death and me? I glanced at the byline —Frieda Appleby—and read on. "Parker was recently elected to his position on the board of selectman, replacing longtime incumbent Meryl Ferguson. His take on town governance has been hotly contested, and his pro-development approach has already seen pushback from longtime locals." Like who? I wondered as I kept reading. Not much more of interest in the article, other than to say that he was survived by his ex-wife, Gretchen Parker, and a brother, Josiah Parker, who was named as a "local fisherman."

No mention of anyone who might have been drinking champagne with him in his bedroom, unfortunately. But the article did mention that local authorities were investigating the case as a homicide.

I groaned and leaned back in my chair, my eyes falling on the copy of Letting Go I'd arranged on the shelf to the left of the front desk just two days ago.

Easier to say than do, for sure.

BETHANY ARRIVED at one o'clock after what had been a busy morning. I'd placed another book order with the distributor for my summer-themed kids' book display, selected a few books for the orders that had come in online (I was still figuring out the web site my friend Ellie had insisted I get designed), and sold a nice mix of fiction and nonfiction to a number of customers... enough to calm some of my fears about not being profitable enough to survive. Although I still had bigger fish to fry, namely whether or not I owned the building.

I also had to say a lot of "I don't know" to the curiosity-seekers who pretended to browse, then accosted me at the counter with questions about Cal Parker before drifting out the door.

"How's it going?" my young assistant asked.

"Well, murder is apparently good for traffic, if not business," I told her.

"I was thinking of putting together that mystery writers' group, but I should hold off on it," she fretted.

"I'd be more worried about that if one of us had actually committed murder," I told her. "The 'free cookie with every purchase' thing seems to be working, but we're getting low on cookies; can you hold down the fort while I head upstairs and whip some more up?"

"Of course," she said.

"And then I have some... business I have to take care of in town."

"I'll look after everything," she said.

I thanked her, then went upstairs and calmed my nerves by clearing the counters and assembling the ingredients for a batch of brown sugar shortbread cookies. As I creamed the sugar and butter together, I found my eye drawn to the rocky shoreline behind the inn. The bar connecting Snug Harbor to Snug Island was covered over by water, but I could still make out the shallow beach beneath the soft waves. An osprey wheeled overhead before circling down to its nest, which looked like a huge bundle of twigs at the top of a half-dead spruce tree on the far end of Snug Island. I was hoping to track down my binoculars soon so I could check for baby ospreys; when I went downstairs, I needed to check the Audubon guide for breeding and fledging times.

As the osprey settled onto its nest, I added flour and salt to the bowl of creamed sugar and butter, then sprinkled brown sugar on a sheet of wax paper, my eyes drifting once more to the beach outside the window. I had just finished rolling the dough in the wax paper and popped it into the fridge when I spotted a woman walking the beach—not near the waterline, where the finds usually are, but further up the shoreline, in an area that was above the tide mark. Something about her was familiar, and there was a furtive aspect to her movement that caught my attention. After squatting down to peer at something on the ground, she turned, staring up at the shop from behind dark glasses before resuming her scan of the beach. As I watched, she stooped and plucked something that resembled a scrap of paper from the rocks, looking at it for a moment before tucking it into her pocket, then glanced up at the store and hurried back the way she'd come.

Abandoning my cookies, I opened the door and rushed down the stairs outside. I got to the end of the walkway and ran onto the beach just as she slipped through the woods several dozen yards down the beach. She wore a black hooded jacket and jeans, along with large sunglasses that obscured her face. I hurried after her and found the narrow path she'd gone up between two large houses. I followed her all the way to Cottage Street, but by the time I got there, she had either ducked into another building or gotten into a car. Although I stood there for a few minutes, scanning passersby, there was no sign of her.

Still thinking, I headed back to Seaside Cottage Books. Was the woman I'd seen just someone out for a walk on the beach, stooping down for a piece of sea glass? Was it the intruder of a few nights past?

Or was it Cal Parker's murderer?

I had been able to tell it was a woman by the flare of her hips; but who? Cal's ex-wife Gretchen? Or the mystery woman from Windswept? Someone had texted him about meeting him; I didn't want to tell the police I'd seen the text, but I knew he'd been late to something. Was it a rendezvous at the beach, or something else? And if she had picked up a piece of paper, was it something that the investigators had missed?

The wheels of my mind were still turning as I returned to my cookie baking. Odds were good the woman wasn't coming back—she appeared to have found what she'd been looking for—but my eyes kept drifting to the shoreline as I washed the bowl and started a batch of raspberry melt-aways; I'd let them bake while the shortbread chilled. I mixed up the sweet vanilla batter and dropped rounds onto two cookie sheets, then made the buttery raspberry filling while the cookies baked in the oven. Finally, when the buttery cookies had cooled enough, I sandwiched them with raspberry cream filling, arranged them on a cake plate, and glanced outside one more time before heading downstairs to the shop, Winston at my heels.

"PROGRESS?" Bethany asked, looking up from the desk, where she was poring over a psychology textbook.

"I've got a batch of cookies done and dough in the fridge, but I've got to do an errand, and I can't take Winston." I looked down at the little white Bichon mix, who was wagging his tail at me hopefully. "Can you keep an eye on him and take the cookies out when the timer goes off? I put a cooling rack on the counter; the other pans are ready to go.

You can put them in for 8 minutes or wait for me to get back, whatever works for you."

"I think I can handle it," she said. "Thank goodness you put the bell on the door!"

I looked up at the ship's bell I'd bought from an antique store in town; it tolled every time someone opened the door. Handy if I was upstairs when a customer came in. Maybe I should put one on the back door to scare off intruders, too, I thought to myself.

"Thanks," I said, feeling confident about leaving the store in her hands as I headed out the door to visit the bane of my existence in Snug Harbor.

If Scooter Dempsey had a copy of a will deeding half of Seaside Cottage Books to Loretta, I wanted to see it.

he afternoon had warmed up, and although I felt a stab of guilt leaving Winston behind, I knew he'd be in good hands with Bethany.

As I walked up Cottage Street, admiring the shop windows of Snug Harbor Souvenirs and Coastal Potters and savoring the feel of the cool ocean breeze on my face, tinged with (once again) that tantalizing whiff of fried clams from the Salty Dog, I checked my phone for Scooter Dempsey's address and oriented myself.

His office was only two blocks off the town green, and it only took ten minutes of walking before I was standing on the sidewalk outside of a brown house with a sign bearing the words DEMPSEY DEVELOPMENT.

Squaring my shoulders and taking a deep breath, I walked through the front door, which opened into a small reception area lined with pictures of horses. Beyond it was a narrow hallway flanked with doors. A small, dented mahogany desk with a bored-looking young man sitting behind it stood to my left. The young man eyed me with minimal interest, then picked up a beeping phone and said,

"Dempsey Development." As he spoke, he twirled a roller-ball pen in his right hand. When he'd pushed the button to forward the call, I smiled at him and said, "I'd like to speak with Scooter."

"Do you have an appointment?" he asked.

"He'll talk to me," I informed him. "I'm Max Sayers."

"Well, I'll tell him you're here," he said, pushing himself back from the desk and strolling down the hallway as if he had all the time in the world.

I took advantage of that time to peruse the desk.

There was a stack of listings for sale, of course, including an eye-popping one for another property on Cottage Street that was selling for three times what I'd spent on Seaside Cottage Books. But there was also an old-fashioned message pad, with those pink "receipt" slips that record the message for posterity.

I glanced at it, looking for something relevant and trying to banish a twinge of conscience. There were several messages from contractors about drafts that hadn't come through. Most of them were marked URGENT. There was a message from CP for Scooter, saying he needed to talk ASAP. Cal Parker? I wondered.

And a message from Agatha Satterthwaite to Scooter, saying she couldn't find something and needed to talk about it RIGHT AWAY. That message was from two days ago... not long before Cal Parker was murdered.

I quickly snapped a photo. I heard a noise down the hallway and stepped back from the desk just as the receptionist reappeared.

"He'll see you in ten minutes," the young man announced and sat back down in a languid movement, then proceeded to clean his fingernails with a paperclip. Crisis averted, at least for now.

I sat in one of the three wooden chairs across from the desk, hearing the low voices of people on phones behind closed doors and wondering how this meeting was going to go. Not well, I imagined.

Twenty minutes passed, during which I had ample time to examine the art above the desk—a painting of Seabiscuit with a jockey astride his back, the horse's name embossed on a brass plate on the frame (which was the only way I knew what horse it was). A second painting, this one of a horse called Blue Moon, hung above my head, matted and framed in heavy, dark wood. Scooter had evidently acquired a passion for horses over the years since last I'd seen him, or else he was trying to project some kind of cultured image.

Finally, Scooter called down the hall that he was free. The receptionist stood up and led me out of the reception area, past a copy room that smelled of burnt coffee and copiers, to a door at the end of the hall. Scooter was there, sitting at a massive desk, wearing the same satisfied smirk I'd seen the other night at the store, more pictures of horses festooning the walls.

"Glad to see you, Max," he'd said. "I hear you made a nasty discovery."

"I did," I confirmed. "Your business partner, yes?"

"Not since he took office, of course, but in the past, yes. Tragic." Scooter didn't look all that broken up about it; his doughy face was impassive, except for those slitty eyes.

"Any idea who might have wanted to do him in?" I asked.

"Who knows?" he shrugged. "We did business, but we weren't close friends. Speaking of business... Come to talk about selling the place?'

"Not exactly," I said, still standing in the doorway.

"No?" His eyebrows rose in an expression of surprise, but

his eyes told me this was just what he'd expected. "Come on in and we'll talk about it. Did Rupert offer you a drink?"

My eyes slid to Rupert, who was standing in the hallway eyeing me with some interest for the first time. "No," I said, "but I'm okay."

"Well, if you change your mind, let me know," Scooter said as I walked into his office, looking at the horse pictures lining the walls, paired with photos of retail developments —evidently projects his company had worked on—and thinking how out of place they'd be in Snug Harbor. His desk was massive and squatted like a mahogany toad in the middle of the room. Behind him was an imposing wall of bookshelves containing encyclopedias, horse books and property code tomes: light reading for a sunny afternoon. His visitors' chairs were small and spindly, all the better to make their occupants feel intimidated when Scooter sank back into his enormous studded leather chair.

"I didn't know you had so much interest in horses," I said, glancing at another painting of the same horse I'd seen above my head in the reception area. "This one in particular, Blue Moon."

"She's my lucky horse, actually," he said, puffing up a bit.

"You own a race horse?" I asked.

"No," he said. "She just made me a lot of money a few years back, so I'm fond of her. But I'm guessing that's not what you're here for. You're going to try to make a go of it with the old bookshop, eh?" he asked, leaning back with his hands behind his head.

"I came because I'd like to see a copy of the will you told me about."

"Ah," he said. "Rupert should be able to put his hands on a copy." He jabbed at the phone on his desk and loudly requested the office manager/receptionist find the necessary paperwork, then jabbed it again and turned his attention back to me. "Still as pretty as ever," he commented.

"Thank you," I said stiffly, the compliment making me feel even more uncomfortable.

"Single again, I understand. That was your ex-husband who was with the author, right? Theodore Sayers: he's a mortgage broker in Boston."

"That's right."

"They looked like regular lovebirds, didn't they? He sure didn't wait long; you've been divorced for less than a year, haven't you? And she's hot, too." When I didn't answer, he said, "I don't know how he let you get away, though."

"I'm sorry," I said. "Is there a point to this line of conversation?"

He shrugged, but didn't look cowed. "I'm just making small talk while we wait for Rupert. I guess you'll be moving in with your mother once this all gets squared away, right?"

"I plan to stay in the store," I told him, folding my arms over my torso.

"I'm sure we can come to some arrangement," he said. "But you'll probably have to get a mortgage. You paid cash for the place, right? Not a smart move, actually, with interest rates being this low."

I didn't like debt, but I wasn't going to tell him anything more than I had to. Obviously, he'd done his research. What else did he know about me?

"I heard you've got some permitting violations going on, too. Although with Cal Parker out of the way, I don't imagine the town will be going after you anytime soon," he added, his mouth quirking up into a suggestive smile. "Convenient, though, isn't it?"

"Could you just check on the documents?" I asked. "I have to get back to the store."

"Of course," he said. "It'll take a minute or two, since they're in the back room. In the meantime, what did you think of our offer?"

"I don't see why I should pay a second time for something when I already signed a contract and paid for it," I said.

"Again, it's just too bad you didn't get a title search," he said, shaking his head. "Trying to save a few bucks; I understand. Pennywise and pound foolish."

Before I could leap across the desk and rip off his head, thankfully, Rupert knocked lightly and appeared in the doorway holding a sheaf of paper. "I think this is what you're looking for," he said.

"Give it here," Scooter told him, and the younger man slid it onto the desk before giving me a suspicious look and disappearing back out through the door. Had he figured out I'd been sorting through the papers on his desk?

"Here's the will deeding the building to both Loretta and Agatha," Scooter said, flipping through the pages before closing them up and sliding the sheaf across the desk to me. "All signed, sealed, and delivered."

I took the papers and looked at them; as he said, the house was split evenly between the sisters, and had been signed and witnessed.

"I don't understand," I said. "If this will is valid, why is Agatha only making noise about it now? Loretta's been running the place for years."

He shrugged. "My understanding is that she was fine with her sister running the store, with the understanding that she'd get half the value of the land and building if it was sold."

"But why do this now?" I said. "Why not address this months ago, when Loretta sold it to me?" And why hadn't

Loretta mentioned that her sister owned half the property? She didn't seem like the type of person who would hide something like that from me, or enter into a transaction that wasn't on the up and up.

I thought about the message from Agatha. What couldn't she find? Something related to the will?

And then a thought popped into my head. Was there another will I didn't know about? One signed after this one?

Scooter, hands still behind his head, leaned back further in his chair and put his feet on the desk, reminding me of a lion claiming his territory. "Be that as it may, as you can see, you don't have clear title to the property. And it doesn't look like anyone registered the new deed." He paused, giving me a conniving look that infuriated me. "Our offer might ease your pain."

"Thanks," I said, "but I need to talk to my attorney."

"Oh, did you hire Nicholas?" he asked, his voice laced with sarcasm. "I didn't know you two were talking."

I couldn't resist. "You mean after what you did all those years ago?"

He widened his eyes. "I don't know what you mean."

"Really," I snorted. "All those rumors you spread about me?"

He spread his hands in mock innocence, but that smirk was still there. "I'm at a total loss."

"Right," I said. "I need a copy of this."

"It's not going to change anything. Rupert!" he called.

Rupert didn't answer; he walked down the hall to look for him. "Must have gone for a coffee break. I guess you can use the copier down the hall." He waved dismissively toward the door. "I've got a meeting in five minutes. Although I'd be happy to discuss this further..." He took his feet off the desk and leaned toward me "...over dinner."

"No thank you," I bit out, repulsed, and headed for the door.

"Be sure to give that back to Rupert," he called after me. "There's a copy filed at the courthouse, but I'd hate to charge you for Rupert's time going over there to copy another one."

I didn't bother answering; I just left the office and headed to the copy room, wrinkling my nose at the smell of old coffee.

I was still riled up as I slapped the papers down on the copier and hit the "start" button. By the time the last page was copied, I'd calmed down some, but I wasn't exactly in a Zen state of mind. I turned through the pages to make sure I had them all; on the sixth page, next to the paragraph deeding the house to both Agatha and Loretta, was a tiny yellow post-it note. All it said was "DDFLD? CKW/AS. NTY?" I looked to see if I had copied the cryptic note. I had.

I was about to leave when I spotted something in the TO BE COPIED box: it was the first page of a will, and the person in question was Loretta Satterthwaite—NOT Loretta and Agatha's mother, Laverne. I picked it up and glanced through it. Everything she had went to charity... not a dime went to her sister.

Was this what had prompted the claim on the property? I wondered.

As I stepped out of the copy room, I heard Scooter's low voice.

"Look again," he was saying. "If we can't put our hands on it, the whole deal is off. I want to help you, you know I do, but it's got to be taken care of." I paused and listened.

"By the end of the week," he said. "I don't want to take any chances." Another silence. "No! Of course I didn't have anything to do with it. Probably some woman he broke up with, crime of passion, and all that." He paused for a moment, then said, "All right. Remember. By the end of the week."

I could hear the click of the phone being hung up, and strode down the hallway to where Rupert was sitting. "Here," I said, handing him the will, then put on my nicest smile and said, "Hey... could you tell me who just called Mr. Dempsey?"

"No," he said flatly. Then, "Have a nice day."

Oh, well. It was worth trying.

I let myself out of his bitter-smelling office and took a deep breath of the cool air, thinking about that note on the will. What did those letters mean, anyway? I had no idea... but I had a feeling if I could figure it out, it would help me understand why Agatha had chosen to stake her claim so suddenly. And what was it that she was looking for that she needed to talk to Scooter about? It made no sense.

And it took me no closer to explaining what had happened to Cal Parker.

As I walked the fresh-scrubbed brick sidewalks toward Main Street, enjoying the cool breeze playing with my hair, my thoughts turned back to the grisly discovery I'd made outside the shop. Already I was getting the impression that not only the police, but ordinary folks in Snug Harbor suspected I had something to do with it. After all, I wasn't totally "local," and he had been found on my property the morning after he'd threatened to shut me down. With my flatiron embedded in his head, no less, although that supposedly wasn't common knowledge.

Whoever Scooter had been talking to had seemed to be asking if he had anything to do with it. He'd denied it... but why would someone think that?

And who were the women Cal had been dating?

I rounded the corner onto Main Street, where I was met

with the flashing stained glass ornaments outside of Snug Harbor Suncatchers, along with the chiming of the clock outside the bank. I caught a whiff of coffee—the delicious, non-burnt variety—and glanced over to Sea Beans, which seemed to be doing a booming business, I was glad to see. Maybe we could serve their coffee at the bookstore? I wondered. I took two more steps and decided coffee was definitely in my immediate future.

Because parked right outside was the green Jaguar I'd seen at Windswept.

he hum of the espresso machine and the chatter of animated voices mingled with the sound of jazz coming from the speakers as I pulled the door to Sea Beans open.

I'd been in the coffee shop a few times before—I was watching my budget, so didn't spend much on food and drink I hadn't made myself these days, but I'd treated myself a couple of times—and today, as always, I was struck by the cheerful, lively vibe of the place. The front case was filled with luscious pastries, including cinnamon rolls, bagels, muffins like the one Denise had brought over yesterday, croissants, and other carbohydrate-infused delights. A young barista at the old-fashioned espresso machine was pulling two shots of espresso, while another woman closer to my age handled the cash register.

I scanned the little shop, which was filled with a delightful hodgepodge of tables and chairs, including four squishy armchairs in the front corner and a couch and love seat toward the back, and I spotted my target immediately. She was facing away from me, at a small table along the back wall, still wearing her sunglasses even though she was inside and facing away from the windows. The pendant diamond in her ear sparkled as she tilted her head to sip from an espresso cup.

Denise wasn't there. I ordered a drip coffee and paid for it, smiling at the barista, then drifted over to the table next to where the mystery woman sat nursing her espresso.

She was an attractive woman—regal, almost—with dark hair pulled back into a loose bun. She wore jeans that looked tailored (if jeans can be tailored), expensive-looking brown suede pumps, and a red silk blouse, her small waist cinched in by a belt. Her phone, nestled in a silver case, lay face-down on the table; she kept picking it up and checking it, as if waiting for something.

I sat at the table next to hers, sipping my coffee and trying to act nonchalant. She took another sip of her espresso, leaving a russet lipstick print on the white cup. I was about to try to engage her in conversation when there was a buzzing sound from the phone on the table. She grabbed for it, her other hand touching her hair with a nervous gesture as she pressed it to her ear.

"What did you find out?" she asked. A moment later, her chin quivered. "Are you sure?" Silence. "I just... I still just can't believe it," she said, swiping at her eyes beneath the dark sunglasses. More silence. "I know," she said in a low voice. "I should have expected it. He was all talk, but I loved him. I... I'm sorry. I have to go."

She jabbed at the phone with a manicured hand and swiped under her sunglasses.

"I'm sorry to disturb you," I said gently. "But are you okay?"

She turned to me and adjusted her glasses; I noticed thick makeup on the side of her face closest to the wall. "I've had a really bad week," she said. "I don't usually break down in public; sorry."

"No need to be sorry," I offered. "Mine's not been so hot, either."

She considered me from behind the dark sunglasses, which dwarfed her heart-shaped face. "Wait. You're the bookstore owner, right?"

"I am," I confirmed.

"So you're... you're the one who found him," she said, leaning in.

"You mean Cal Parker?"

She nodded. "I... I was seeing him," she said, and she took a deep breath. "I just can't believe he's gone."

"I'm so, so sorry," I said. "What an awful thing to happen."

Her lower lip trembled. "He... he was murdered, right?"

I nodded.

"How?"

"I'm not supposed to say," I said.

"Was it... well, quick?"

"It looked like it," I said. "I hate to ask this, but... do you have any idea who might have wanted to do something like that to him?"

She bit her lip. "From what I've heard, it could be you."

"It's not," I assured her. "Trust me. I only met him the first time the night before. I could never do anything like that to another person." Besides, I added silently, if I were going to do in anyone, it would be Agatha Satterthwaite. Or Scooter Dempsey.

"I want to know what happened, too. I... I was with him that night."

"You were?" I asked, although I already suspected as much.

"We had champagne... it was my birthday. And then we

got into an argument, and I told him I didn't love him, and now..." she sobbed. "Now I'll never see him again so I can't tell him I didn't mean it."

"That's awful," I said, reaching out to touch her hand. She grabbed onto my hand as if it were a life preserver and she were a drowning woman surrounded by hungry sharks. "So what happened after the argument? Did he go out for a walk?"

"I don't know," she said. "I left right after we fought. And now... I keep thinking that if I'd stayed, maybe he wouldn't be dead."

"Nothing you did or didn't do had anything to do with what happened to Cal Parker," I said. "If someone really meant to do this, they would have found a way."

"You think?" she asked.

"Yes," I confirmed, using the same tone of voice I used to talk my kids through their self-doubt.

"I'm Deirdre, by the way," she said. "Deirdre Sloane."

"Max Sayers," I said. "Good to meet you, although I'm sorry about the circumstances."

"Me too," she said forlornly.

"I know it's hard, but the thing now is to figure out what happened, so whoever did it doesn't kill again."

"What do you mean? You think someone else might die?"

"I don't know," I said. "I don't know why someone killed Cal. Do you have any ideas?" I asked a second time.

She lifted her sunglasses slightly to dab at her eyes, and I suddenly understood why she wore the glasses inside— and why she had applied such heavy makeup to her already smooth skin.

Even through the pancake make-up, I could see an ugly purple bruise blossoming under her eye.

"Why would someone want to kill him?"

I shrugged. "Did he make life difficult for anyone?"

She snorted. "Just about everyone in Snug Harbor, it seems like. He wanted change. Nobody likes change."

"What kind of change?"

"Modern, standardized business procedures," she said. "Making sure the town was profitable. There were a lot of old-timers who wanted things to be just like they always were. Not come into the 21st century, you know?"

"Like who?"

"Well, the guy from the Salty Dog was livid with him for cracking down on code violations. He came to the house last week and said Cal should be run out of town on a rail. Or worse."

"Ouch," I said.

"And then there was that woman he beat in the election. Meryl? She tried to chat me up last week, find out dirt on Cal. Her family's been on the board of selectmen since Snug Harbor started. She saw him as a usurper."

"Do you think she'd kill him over it?"

Deirdre shrugged. "You never know what people will do," she said in an odd, dreamy voice.

"This is an awkward question," I said, pausing to sip my coffee, "but do you know who inherits Cal's estate?"

She looked away quickly and said, in a flat tone, "No."

I didn't believe her.

"Do you think he might have willed it to his brother?" I pressed.

"No way," she said quickly. "He would have been happy if Josiah left town and never came back."

"Why?"

"Josiah is a jerk," she said. "Always asking for money, when he didn't do anything to earn it. They came from a middle-class background, you know. Cal was a self-made man. Josiah had every opportunity he had—more, in fact. Their parents paid for Josiah to go to a fancy prep school, but not Cal, did you know that? Josiah was the family's golden boy."

"It didn't turn out that way, though, did it?"

"It certainly didn't," she said, turning her espresso cup around with a pale hand. No engagement or wedding ring on the third finger, I noticed. "I admire... admired his drive," she said. "He always got what he wanted, and wouldn't stop until he won."

"Do you think that may have been what happened? He pushed someone and they pushed back?"

Her hands tightened on the cup; the knuckles paled. Had I touched a nerve?

"Maybe," she said, then released the cup and checked her phone again. "It's been nice talking to you—thanks for listening—but I've got to go."

"Feel free to drop by the store anytime," I said. "And if you need anything..."

"Right. Thanks again," she said, and gathered up her Coach purse and strode to the front of the shop, leaving her espresso cup behind.

As she pushed through the door, I wondered who she'd been talking to before I struck up a conversation with her.

And why she hadn't told me who *had* inherited Cal Parker's estate.

Because I would have bet one of the last dollars I owned that Deirdre knew.

"How'd it go?" I asked Bethany as I walked through the front door of Seaside Cottage Books a half hour after, taking a deep breath and savoring the scent of books, floor polish, fresh cookies, and fresh outside air. I'd stopped at the grocery store to pick up supplies for dinner along the way, and was carrying two grocery bags. Winston trotted over to greet me, standing up on his hind legs to inspect the grocery bags and say hello. I normally discouraged this behavior, but today my heart warmed at the welcome, and he half-closed his brown eyes in ecstasy as I rubbed the top of his head.

"Another seventy-five dollars in sales," she said brightly. "And those cookies are a hit!"

"Good," I said. The cake dish I'd set up next to the register was filled with what was left of the raspberry melt-away cookies; I'd made. "There's shortbread dough in the fridge upstairs; I'll toss those cookies in soon."

"Sounds yummy," she said. "But I want that raspberry cookie recipe."

"Of course," I told her. "Anything exciting to report?"

"I don't know if it's exciting," she said, picking up a slip of paper from the desk. "But Nicholas called."

"Oh," I said, trying to sound nonchalant. I guess I hadn't given him my cell number, so he'd called the store. "Thanks. I'm going to run upstairs and give him a call back."

"I'll be here," she said, but I thought I saw her lips twitch up into a little smile as I hurried up the stairs.

Winston followed me up the stairs. I closed the door to the store, grabbed a piece of cheese from the fridge for my fluffy friend, took a deep breath, and dialed the number. A woman with a professional voice answered, and connected me to Nicholas.

"Hey," I said. "Max here."

"I'm sorry I called the store; I realized I didn't have your number."

"No worries," I said. "I'll give it to you now." Feeling a flutter of excitement, I reeled off my number. "Sorry again about the coffee incident. I owe you one."

"I ran into you," he reminded me. "Anyway, I'm sorry to have to be the bearer of bad tidings, but..."

"Oh, no," I said, sinking down onto a card-table chair. "I'm sitting down. Lay it on me."

"The only will recorded gave the store to both sisters," he said.

"There wasn't another one?"

"If so, it wasn't recorded," he said. "And I can't find anything else recorded that would forfeit Agatha's right to the property."

"Uh oh. Which means..."

"That unless you can come up with some kind of evidence to disprove it, Agatha's claim is valid."

15

"*E*vidence," I said, leaning back as I took in what he'd told me. "What kind of evidence?'

"A different will, a deed; anything that shows that Loretta was the property's sole owner when the transaction took place. Hopefully you registered the deed?"

"I don't know that we did," I said, "but I'll look. I'm confused, though; why would Agatha be complaining about this now, and not years ago, when Loretta took over the shop? Or when she sold it to me?"

"There is something odd about the timing," he agreed. "But without a piece of paper showing that Loretta owned the property outright, Agatha's got a good claim."

I leaned back, feeling drained. "What do I do?"

"I'd talk to some of Loretta's friends. Find out if she mentioned anything about a transaction between Agatha and Loretta. Or if she had a safe deposit box we don't know about... anything that might turn up something in your favor."

"I can't believe she'd take money for a property that wasn't hers."

"From what I knew of her, I can't either," he said. "But people do funny things."

"They do, don't they?" I asked. "Hey... are wills public knowlege?"

"Are you thinking of Cal Parker?"

"Yeah. I normally wouldn't ask about something like that, but I'm worried I might be a suspect, and I'm wondering who would benefit from his death."

"Hmm. It's early for the will to be probated, but I'll see what I can find out."

"Thank you," I said. "I really appreciate your help... can I cook dinner for you sometime?"

There was a long silence during which I cursed myself for my forwardness.

"Ah, let me think on that."

"Oh. Okay. Sorry if I kind of overstepped..."

"No, no, it's okay. Hey... I've got another call. Can I catch up with you later?"

"Sure," I said, feeling a rush of embarrassment. "And thanks again."

"No problem," he said, and as he hung up, I resisted the urge to bang my head against the wall repeatedly.

"Nice going, Max," I said to myself. Not only had I presumed that his services were free, I'd done something that sounded like asking him for a date. When he hadn't spoken with me for decades and things were just starting to warm up again.

And then there was the fact that I'd spent everything I had to buy a building that apparently now didn't belong to me.

I needed a break from reality, I thought as I stood up, Winston looking at me questioningly—he always knew when I was upset—and trudged back downstairs.

Thank goodness I lived above a book store.

"What's going on?" Bethany asked as I emerged from my rooms looking rather like the walking dead. "You look like you got hit by a truck up there."

"More or less."

"But sales have been so good! And the opening night was a huge success."

"I know," I said. "But Agatha's still going after the store." I told her the details.

"Still?"

"Yup," I said. "And unless I can prove her wrong, there's nothing I can do."

"It makes no sense at all," she said. "You know who you need to talk to? Miriam Culpepper."

"Who's that?"

"She's Loretta's next door neighbor. They had tea every Wednesday; she grew up with Agatha and Loretta." She wrote down the woman's name and address and handed it to me. "Any word on what happened to Cal?"

"Nothing yet," I said, "and they haven't been by to arrest me, so that's some good news. Have you heard any rumors about him? Or his romantic life?"

"He's been seeing some woman for the last year or so, apparently—I don't know if he still is, or was at the time of his death; but he was a few months ago—but they don't really go out in public together. I don't know why. Maybe she wouldn't be good for him politically?"

"Then why would she be there?"

I shrugged. "I don't know."

"Do you know anything else about her?"

"I know she drives a nice car, but that's only because a friend of mine works for a catering company that did his party when he won the selectman position."

"Who?" I asked.

"Dining Downeast," she said. "I'll ask her when I see her at class."

"Great," I said. "Any other talk around town about who might have wanted to kill him?"

She averted her eyes.

"They still think it's me?"

"Well, it was right by the store," she said, "and it was your flatiron."

I sighed. "Have the police been by anymore?"

"Not yet," she said, in a tone of voice that didn't inspire confidence.

Great.

I sighed. "Thanks for letting me know. I'll see if I can get in touch with Miriam to see what she can tell me about Agatha. In the meantime, why don't you head out for the afternoon? I'll take care of the store."

"Are you sure?" she asked. "I'm trying to get this chapter finished today."

"Go," I said. "Winston and I will hold down the fort."

"Okay. But call me if you need me!" Bethany slung her backpack over one shoulder and headed out the door, and as I watched her go, I found myself grateful once again that she had come into my life. As I looked around me at the colorful books filling the shelves, with Bethany's hand-lettered signs marking the different genres, I felt a warm upwelling. I hoped the two of us could find a way to make a go of the store.

My eye was drawn again to the shelf that the intruder had attacked the other night. I walked over, wondering what whoever it was had been looking for when they started pulling away the shelves. Was something hidden in the store somewhere? And if so, who had hidden it? Loretta, or whoever had owned the store before her?

I felt the edge that had been pulled away. There was nothing behind it, but what about the other shelves?

I walked from shelf to shelf, moving the books away and knocking gently on the wood, listening for a hollow sound. I had made it through Religion, Nature, Self Help and Cooking when the bell rang. I put the books back on the shelf, feeling self-conscious, and turned to greet whoever had walked in the door.

It was a woman I didn't recognize; she gave me a shy smile and headed over to the fiction section, where she selected a few Maeve Binchy books, and then she got a cross-stitch guide from the craft section.

"Find what you needed?" I asked as she put her treasures on the counter.

"I always love Maeve Binchy," she said. "I'm so glad you took over the shop. I miss Loretta, of course, but I knew she was happy with you taking it over. And I love what you've done with the place. Did you make the pillows on the chairs yourself?"

"I did!" I told her. "Thank you so much for noticing!"

"I bought some of the same fabric for a quilt for my granddaughter," she told me. "I just love the bright colors; I know Loretta would have loved it, too."

"Did you know Loretta well?" I asked as I rang up her purchases.

"We were in elementary school together," she told me.

"Really! You knew each other a whole lifetime, then."

"We did," she said, nodding. "I'm Miriam Culpepper, by the way."

"Oh! Bethany just told me about you; I was just going to look you up! I'm Max Sayers," I said. "Lovely to meet you."

"Likewise, and I'm so glad you have the store. Like I said, I've known Loretta almost all my life, and if she picked you, there's a reason." She gave me a smile that warmed my heart.

"And you know her sister, Agatha, too?"

"Oh, Aggie. Always jealous of her sister. Their father always favored Loretta... she was the oldest, and ever so clever in school. Aggie never could keep up, and she resented the heck out of her big sister."

"Did they ever make up?"

"After her mother died, Loretta told me she tried to make things right with her sister. That's what she said to me, anyway... I don't know what she meant. And it worked for a while, but there at the end, Agatha was after her again."

"When she was sick?" I asked.

Miriam nodded. "Aggie started making noise about how she didn't get her fair share. That Loretta had duped her out of what she deserved, and that she'd find a way to get it back."

"What did she mean by that?" I asked.

"I don't know," she said, "but I think it had something to do with the house. That was what their parents had left to give " She looked at me. "The girls were both raised here, you know. Loretta was the one who turned it into a bookstore once her parents weren't able to stay there anymore; I'm pretty sure she used some of the profits to help her mother and father pay the bills."

"That sounds like Loretta," I said, thinking of the kindly woman with a love of traditional mysteries who had introduced me to Agatha Christie, Diane Mott Davidson, Sara Paretsky, and countless other amazing authors. "And I'm so glad she did. Every town needs a bookstore."

"You're absolutely right."

"How sad that it caused a breach between the sisters, though," I said. "Money can do terrible things to family, can't it?"

"Never had much myself," the woman said, "but the stories I've heard... like what happened between Cal Parker and his brother, Josiah. Tragic, what happened to Cal, by the way. I still don't think he made a good selectman, but nobody should go that way. And so young! I'm sorry you had to be the one to find him."

"It was a shock," I admitted. "Do you think his brother had something to do with it?"

She considered the question for a moment before answering. "Josiah's jealous of his brother's success," Miriam said. "Same thing as Aggie and Loretta, really. Josiah always felt he got a bum deal, despite the fact that his family gave him more advantages starting out. I hate to think he would have, but people do odd things."

"I've never met Josiah, but I can see it would be hard having such a successful sibling."

"Oh, but you did meet him," she said. "I saw you sell him a book the night of the grand opening."

"You were here? I'm so sorry I don't remember! What does he look like, anyway?"

"Bearded, a bit unkempt. Nothing remarkable, although he resembles his brother."

I searched my memory, but I'd been so preoccupied with Scooter—not to mention my ex and his author girlfriend and my old summer crush—that I didn't recall him. "I don't remember him at all," I said.

"You had your hands full that night. I'd love the recipe for those coconut cookies if you have it, though. And those look mighty good, too," she said, pointing to the few raspberry cookies left on the cake plate.

"Thanks for reminding me. Free cookie with every purchase!" I said, grabbing a napkin and lifting the lid. "These came out of the oven a few hours ago. I'll give you the biggest one," I told her.

"I shouldn't have it, but..." She took the cookie and sank her teeth into it. "Mmmm. Delicious," she mumbled through a mouthful of crumbs. "If you get tired of selling books, you should consider opening a bakery."

I laughed. "I love them both."

As she turned to go, she paused, swallowing her mouthful of cookie. "Did Loretta ever tell you about the history of this place?"

"No," I said, shaking my head. "I know the house was in the family for a long time, but I've only ever known it as Seaside Cottage Books."

"It used to be where the town midwife and healer lived," she said. "Loretta's great-great-grandmother had a wall full of books upstairs. If you were expecting, or cut yourself on a hook, or came down with the sniffles, you came to see Mrs. Muriel. She had a garden of healing herbs in the back— Loretta told me that a few odd herbs still pop up now and again—and she practiced out of the front room. The wealthy folks went to see the doctor, but if you didn't have the money or trusted in the old ways more than the new, you came here."

"Wow," I said, looking around me at the book-lined walls. I wondered, not for the first time, how many stories this house had seen over the years. "Anyone else of interest?"

"Well, rumor has it her grandfather was quite an important man around here during Prohibition," she said. I don't know if you know it or not, but Snug Harbor was THE place to summer for the wealthy. And the wealthy liked their liquor. Which Loretta's grandfather was happy to provide."

"Loretta's grandfather was a rumrunner?"

"It was never proven, but he had quite a network. This house was where everything was stashed; ever wonder why the cellar is bigger than the house?"

"I hadn't, really, but you're right." I'd only been down there a few times, to check the boiler; it was damp down there, and totally unsuitable for books.

"Loretta told me she never found much to show for it, though," Miriam said. "Broken glass here and there, but not much else."

"So no buried treasure?"

"Not exactly, no. Rumor has it that the stash was kept on Snug Island somewhere, and late at night, they'd ferry it over in a small boat and hide it here for distribution."

"We're right up the road from the restaurants," I said. "Was this some kind of business at the time?"

"It was just a house then," she said. "In fact, I'm not sure Loretta's grandmother knew what her husband was up to. She was the staunchest anti-liquor campaigner in town. No one realized it was her husband who was in charge of the whole network until he got caught red-handed."

"What happened?"

"Coast Guard was tipped off. He was found in a lobster boat whose entire hull was filled with cases of gin."

"Ouch."

"Thing is, he was careful. Wasn't a big spender, and no one knows where the money went."

"Maybe the cellar?"

"Maybe," she said. "Rumor had it he had a leather book where he kept all his accounts in some kind of code. The story also says it's got directions to where he hid his ill-gotten gains."

"A treasure map?"

"That's what they say," she said. "Of course, that was a hundred years ago, and there have been generations of Satterthwaites in this house since and nobody's ever found it." She cocked her head to one side. "I thought maybe with all the renovations you were doing, maybe you might run across it; I didn't want you to throw it out."

"Other than a few old medicine bottles and the sole of a shoe, I haven't found anything like that," I said, thinking of the odds and ends I'd found in a corner of the cellar. "I'll keep an eye out, though, even though I'm sure it's just a figment of someone's imagination."

"Maybe. Maybe not." She took the books, tucking them into her tote bag, and thanked me again. "Good luck to you, and let me know if you do find anything. And if you see any other books you think I might like, please drop me a line."

"I will," I told her. "And thank you for your support."

"Of course," she said. "I'll see you soon. And don't get into any more trouble!" she advised me.

"I'll try not to," I told her.

THE REST of the afternoon was quiet in the store, so I was able to spend some time in between customers on unpacking and arranging my kitchen. By the time I closed the shop and headed upstairs for the night, the little cafe table and chairs were clear of boxes, I'd tied back the white curtains over the sink, I'd laid out my favorite blue Provençal tablecloth, and even had time to run down and snip a few roses from the bushes outside the store to fill a Mason jar.

I had decided to make myself one of my favorite healthy comfort foods, an Italian pasta dish featuring arugula, lemons, and cherry tomatoes and a yummy local goat cheese they carried at the grocery store. For dessert, I'd picked up some fresh blueberries and a pint of vanilla ice cream. I was in the mood for a blueberry buckle a la mode, but didn't have the energy. Even just blueberries and creamy ice cream sounded divine.

I played a Celtic music station on my little portable speaker, filling my new home with soothing music, and while a pot of salted water heated on the stove, I sliced up the cherry tomatoes and peeled garlic, enjoying the homey task of meal preparation. When the water was boiling, I added the pasta, then heated a knob of butter mixed with good olive oil in a pan; soon, I was inhaling the delightful aroma of garlic browning in butter. Before the garlic had a chance to get too dark, I tossed in halved cherry tomatoes; while they cooked, I cut the goat cheese into chunks, rinsed the arugula, and squeezed two lemons into a bowl.

It took only a few minutes to mix everything together; I tossed the cooked pasta into the pan with the tomatoes, then quickly added some reserved pasta water and the arugula and turned off the heat, stirring until the arugula was wilted. Then I added the goat cheese, lemon juice, and a touch of salt and pepper, tasting it until it was perfect.

With a glass of inexpensive Pinot Grigio I poured myself from the bottle in the fridge, it was a satisfying dinner. Although I enjoyed it with my James Herriot book, losing myself, at least for a few minutes, in the Yorkshire Dales with young veterinarian James and his cast of delightful two-legged and four-legged characters, I found myself glancing out the mullioned glass kitchen door at the changing sky. Through the open window, I could hear the lap of the water against the rocks, soothing and time-less. I'd loved living in Boston, but there was something magical about Maine, particularly the coast. Was it possible that I'd find a way to stay here? I certainly hoped so.

I returned to my book, trying to push gloomy thoughts out of my head. With my Italian dinner, Celtic music, and English reading material, I was having a very international evening, I reflected as I popped another tomato into my mouth. As I finished another chapter, I looked around the little kitchen with satisfaction.

The kitchen's walls were bright white, setting off the warmth of the pine cabinets and the blue-and-white hand-painted tiles somebody had installed as a backsplash. It was a small space, with just enough room for the basics and a small table, but something about it told me it had been used lovingly by cooks for many years. Through a wide doorway I could see the living room, where I'd pushed my white slip-covered couch into place, flanking it with two blue armchairs I'd rescued from my study in Boston. At some point I'd get a television. But since I lived above a bookstore, I wasn't sure it was necessary, really.

I'd just cleaned up from dinner and put the leftovers in the fridge when my cell phone rang.

"How are you doing?" Denise asked as I picked up my cell.

"Not great news about the bookstore, but at least no one's arrested me. Yet, anyway." I told her what I'd learned about the deed situation today. Like Bethany, she seemed dispirited, but didn't share it with me.

"I'm sure you'll figure it out," she said, trying to sound optimistic. "I found out a little tidbit today, and I thought I'd share it with you."

"What?" I asked.

"Gretchen Parker was at Scooter Dempsey's office today," she said. "She accused him of helping Cal hide money."

16

"*H*ow do you know that?" I asked.

"One of the baristas heard them through the open window when he went out to his car to get a sweater," she said. "Apparently she was so loud practically the whole street could hear them."

"Interesting," I said. "What prompted that, do you think?"

"Maybe something about Cal's will? I don't know. The divorce is done... you'd think that would be ancient history by now."

"Maybe," I said. "But that stuff lingers... maybe his death just stirred it up."

"Maybe," Denise said, but she didn't sound convinced.

I hung up the phone, still thinking about Gretchen Parker, and busied myself filling Winston's food bowl before he started throwing it around the kitchen floor. He scarfed down his kibble in no time flat, and I leashed him up and put on my walking shoes. Together we stepped out onto the back porch into the cooling evening air. I wasn't sure I was ready to go back down to the beach just yet, but I had to do it eventually. Besides, I told myself, maybe there was a clue the police had missed. And maybe I'd catch a glimpse of the woman I'd seen yesterday.

I kept Winston well clear of the place I'd found Cal's body, scanning the rocky shore as we walked. Winston seemed unconcerned, more focused on the lone sea gull who hadn't found a place to roost for the night (if that's what they did—where did they go, anyway? I wondered briefly). I found nothing out of the ordinary... just a piece of styrofoam cup that I picked up to throw away, and a gazillion mussel shells that glinted blackish-blue in the fading light.

A cool breeze was kicking up as we walked the beach; the tide was going out, exposing the sand bar, and I scanned the darkness under the trees on Snug Island. Apparently there had once been a few houses over there, but they'd been torn down decades ago, and nobody lived there now. Occasionally someone got stuck on the wrong side of the water, or a few people got brave and decided to camp, but except for day trippers and the occasional intrepid backpacker, the ospreys were the only ones I knew who lived there.

As I walked, the breeze riffled my hair. I walked past the backs of a few houses and shops, the grass sloping down to the coast, and then the well-lit shoreline restaurants, the smell of cooking lobster and melted butter and rolls drifting down to Winston and me as we made our way down the beach. The juxtaposition of the dark, wild island just across the water to my left and the happy burble of voices and clang of dishes up on the restaurants' lit decks made me feel strangely adrift between wilderness and community.

This was my home now, I thought to myself. And I was going to do everything I could to make sure it stayed that way.

As Winston and I climbed over a jumble of boulders, I heard the sound of angry voices.

"I don't believe you," a woman's voice said.

"I promise, sweetheart. I had nothing to do with it."

"Then where did you go that night? I know you weren't at home."

"Josiah called," the man said. "I went to his place to have a few beers. I promise. That's all."

"Sure," the woman said, her voice heavy with sarcasm. "I've told you a million times that nothing happened between Cal and me, but you never believed me."

"Let's not drag this up again," he said.

"I have to," she said in a husky voice. "I have to know that you had nothing to do with what happened to Cal. I... I can't live with a murderer."

"A murderer?" The anger in the man's voice made the hair rise on the back of my neck. "If you don't believe that I didn't touch a hair on that scumbag's head..."

"But he was going to ruin our business! And the whole bar heard you threaten to kill him just last week!"

"I swear I didn't kill him," he repeated.

The woman made a choking noise, and I heard the sounds of footsteps.

"Sylvia! Come back!"

I peeked over the boulder, watching as they ran down the beach, her running unevenly, him sprinting to catch up. It must be Jared and Sylvia Berland, the owners of the Salty Dog.

I looked down at Winston, who had spent the time sniffing dried kelp. "Good boy," I told him, thankful he had remained quiet.

Had Jared Berland killed Cal Parker?

And, I wondered with a feeling of foreboding, was Sylvia Berland in danger?

I WAITED for the couple to disappear before continuing on my walk, thinking about the exchange I'd just overheard, and wondering who else Cal Parker had angered enough to threaten him with murder. Although several tourist families walked by with ice cream, I resisted the urge to head up to Stewart's Scoops, instead turning back toward the shop once the path curved toward town. The sun continued to drop as Winston and I picked our way among the rocks, heading back home. The first stars were starting to twinkle above as we walked, mussel shells crunched under my sneakers as we found our way back. Soon, we left the busy restaurants behind, and the windows of the cottage book shop glowed invitingly as we turned up the short path away from the beach. Whatever happened, I felt a rush of gratitude that I was here at this moment.

I took my shoes off next to the door, enjoying the homey, lingering scents of garlic and butter, and settled Winston in with a treat as I headed downstairs to double-check the locks. The front door was bolted tight, as were the windows, and I double-checked the back door before scurrying back up the stairs to my cozy retreat.

Once I slid the deadbolt of the upstairs cottage apartment, I filled the clawfoot tub with warm water and Epsom salts, added a few drops of lavender oil, and retrieved my James Herriot book. By ten, I was tucked into my freshly made bed with a cup of chamomile tea on one side of me and Winston snuggled in on the other, trying to put the worries of the day behind me.

It was eleven by the time I reached over to turn off the light and drifted off to sleep.

I was in the middle of a dream involving Agatha Satterthwaite chasing me into the ocean with an enormous flatiron in her hand when there was a tinkle of glass from somewhere in the cottage.

I sat up straight. Beside me, Winston had also woken up, and he was vibrating with a low growl.

I shushed him and listened. There was silence for several minutes, and then I heard the creak of a floorboard from somewhere below me.

The hairs stood up on my arms; unless I was imagining things, my intruder was back.

closed Winston into the bedroom, tossing him a dental chew to keep him busy, and tiptoed into the kitchen, pulling a knife from the block next to the sink. It glinted in the faint light from the moon outside the window as I crept to the door, opened it slowly, and peered down the stairwell into the darkness.

A flicker of light, as if from a flashlight, danced across the floor at the base of the stairs, and I heard heavy breathing. I grabbed my cell phone to call the police, but then I stopped. What if the intruder would be gone by the time they got to the shop? I really wanted to know who was breaking in—and what they were looking for.

I tiptoed to the bottom of the stairs, the knife tight in my hand. I turned the corner to encounter a shadowy figure bent over my desk, rifling through the drawers.

I took a step closer, hoping to see who it was. I was about to edge to the side, where I might get a chance to see the intruder's face, when Winston burst out in a volley of barks from above me. The intruder turned the flashlight toward the base of the stairs, the light flashing over me as he or she turned, then jerked it back to focus on me.

I squinted into the light, shielding my eyes. "Who are you and what do you want?" I croaked over the cacophony of Winston's barking from upstairs.

No answer. We remained frozen in a stand-off. Then the figure the figure moved. In a split second I saw the glint of the glass paperweight they snatched up from the desk to hurl at me and I ducked, but the heavy globe glanced off my temple, and a burst of pain shot through my head. As I raised my hand instinctively to my head, the intruder rushed past me, pushed through the back door, and fled into the night.

I took a moment to clear my vision, then ran to the back door, knife still in hand, and stared out at the path to the ocean. The flashlight was bouncing—my intruder was running—and as whoever it was turned right and disappeared into the night, I flipped on the lights and looked down at the door. The doorframe was intact, but one of the windows was broken; it looked like someone had smashed the pane and reached in to unlock the door. I relocked the back door, not that it was going to make any difference, and walked to the front of the shop; the door was still locked.

I turned to the desk. The intruder hadn't had much time, but he or she had made the most of it; papers were strewn all over the floor, including the letter regarding the Satterthwaite will, and the bottom drawer was out and upside-down on top of the desk, as if someone was looking at the drawer itself. I thought of the bookshelf that had been slightly pulled out the other day; it was as if someone was looking for some kind of secret compartment or something.

But why?

I grabbed the phone and called the police to let them

know of the break-in, telling them that I was unharmed (except for a small goose egg on my right temple). Once they assured me they were on their way, I headed upstairs to toss on jeans and a T-shirt, threw a few ice cubes in a baggie and wrapped it in a dish towel to make a cold compress and went back downstairs, holding the ice to my forehead and contemplating the drawer lying askew on top of the desk.

Someone was looking for something they thought was hidden in the shop. And it was important enough to break in and pull things apart to look at.

But why?

And why the sudden urgency? I'd been in and out of town for months, with plenty of opportunities to break into the store while no one was in residence. Was Loretta the keeper of some secret treasure, or first-edition book that hadn't been unearthed yet? Had someone just realized it was here? There was a small section of signed first editions on a shelf near the front of the store. I hadn't researched all of them yet, but I hadn't noticed anything that seemed to be of particular value. There were certainly no Gutenberg Bibles among the collection, which largely consisted of first editions by crime writers (one genre preference Loretta and I had had in common).

I headed back to the desk, stymied, and noticed a scrap of paper on the floor. I bent down to look at it; it was a crumpled receipt from the IGA, from 4:37 that afternoon, for a box of mothballs.

I hadn't bought mothballs. And I hadn't seen the receipt when I went up to bed, either. I made a note to point it out to the police when they arrived.

As I continued to prowl around the store, looking for other things out of place, blue and red lights flashed in the windows at the front of the store. A moment later, the detective who had printed me stepped up onto the front porch with a woman I didn't recognize in her wake; her nametag said A. Ramirez. I greeted her, opening the door and thanking her for coming.

She gave me a cool nod. "Detective Ramirez: You must be Max Sayers. Can you tell me what happened?"

I recounted the events of the previous half hour and led her to the desk, then showed her the broken window.

"Was the door unlocked?" she asked.

"It must have been; whoever it was threw the door open and took off. Someone broke in the other night, too, and pulled back part of the bookshelf; with everything that happened on the beach, I forgot to bring it up."

"You forgot," she said in a flat tone, and took a note. Then she inspected the door. "The window pane is right above the lock, but whoever did this must have had a really small hand."

I looked at the hole in the glass; I hadn't noticed it before, but it was a jagged gap not much larger than an apple. "I see what you mean," I said. "Maybe they used a lever or something?"

"Why not just make the hole a little bigger so you could fit your hand through, then?" she asked. "What time did you hear the glass break?"

"I'm not sure," I said, glancing at my watch. "It must have been about thirty minutes ago. It woke Winston and me up. I was about to go back to sleep when I heard more noise, so I decided to come downstairs and investigate."

"Why didn't you call us right away?"

"I should have," I admitted, "but I wanted to see who it was. And I was afraid by the time you got here, whoever it was would be long gone. I grabbed a knife from the kitchen block, just in case." I told her what had happened when the intruder spotted me, and pointed to the glass paperweight that had slid across the floor, coming to rest next to a display of journals. Then I pulled the bag of ice away from my temple to show her where the paperweight had hit me.

"You're lucky a goose egg is all you've got," she said. "You should probably get that checked out though. Make sure you don't have a concussion." She walked over and picked up the glass paperweight. "No blood, and it didn't shatter."

"My head seems to have absorbed most of the force."

"Mmmm," she said doubtfully. "We'll check it for prints, of course."

"You'll likely find mine and Bethany's," I told her.

"Bethany?" she asked.

"My employee," I said.

"Right." She peered at the swelling on my temple. "You really should go to the emergency room,"

"You're probably right," I said, but I'd decided that unless I started having symptoms other than a wicked headache, it would have to wait until tomorrow. I didn't need a $400 emergency room bill at the moment.

"And the desk was like this when you came down?" Detective Ramirez asked, examining the drawer.

"It was," I said. "And whoever it was pulled part of this bookshelf backing away the other day, too. It's almost like they were looking for some kind of secret compartment."

"Secret compartment?" she asked, her tone dubious. "Are you suggesting someone was searching for a secret treasure?"

"I have no idea," I said. "This house is more than a hundred years old; I don't know most of its history. Maybe someone heard an old story about something hidden inside."

"But the desk isn't part of the house," she pointed out.

"It came with the cottage," I told her. "I don't know how long it's been here; it could be original to the house. Like I said, though, I'm just speculating. I have no idea why someone broke in and started rifling through my store."

"Assuming someone broke in at all," she said.

I blinked. "What are you saying?"

"I printed you when you found a dead body. Since that time, you tell me there was a break-in you conveniently forgot to mention. Now you tell me about a break-in that occurred this evening. You didn't call until after the intruder had left, and the hole in the glass seems small."

"Are you suggesting I manufactured the story?" I asked. "What would I possibly have to gain by saying someone broke into my store?"

"I have no idea," Detective Ramirez said. "Publicity? Maybe to throw confusion into a murder investigation? Make it look like someone was after you, instead of Selectman Parker?"

"How would manufacturing a break-in confuse a murder investigation?" I asked. "I can't even see how those two things might possibly be related."

"The murder occurred behind your store. The supposed break-ins occurred at your store."

"*Supposed* break-ins?"

"According to you, the intruder wore gloves, so there won't be any fingerprint evidence. You conveniently 'forgot' to tell me about the first break-in. Tonight, you tell me someone broke a window to let themselves in, but the hole isn't big enough to put a hand through to turn the deadbolt."

"There's a receipt on the floor that wasn't here when I went up to bed." I pointed to the crumpled bit of paper. "It's from this afternoon, at around 4:30."

"Oh?" she asked. "What's it for? Lockpicks? Safe-cracking tools?"

"Mothballs," I said, blushing.

"Right," she said, squatting down and picking up the receipt with gloved hands. "We'll bag it, but it's hardly incriminating."

"I get it," I said. "You're saying I made all this up. Broke my own window to fake an intruder. Upended my desk drawer and messed with one of my bookshelves. And hit myself in the head with a paperweight."

"It's a theory," she said dryly.

"Then why? What's my motive?"

"I don't know. My best guess is that you believed it might muddy the murder investigation. When in fact," she said, "it's just made me more suspicious."

"Of me?" I asked. "I've been living in town for what... two, three days now? And I'm a suspect?'

"Your dealings with Mr. Parker were less than ideal," she pointed out. "And from what I understand, you invested pretty much everything in this business, and his actions put that at risk." She stared at me, and there was a hardness in her eyes that made my stomach churn. "People have killed for less."

"I am not a murderer," I said flatly, grabbing Winston, who had started to growl at the detective, and hugging him to my chest. "And I did not 'fake' a break-in. Someone was looking for something in my shop. And if you're not going to look for the culprit, then I'll have to."

"I'd advise you to avoid interfering in the investigation any further," Detective Ramirez said in a cool voice, her eyes stony. "We'll continue the investigation."

"Thank you," I said politely, if coldly. "If you don't mind, I'm going to go and get a cup of tea. You and your team are welcome to a cup if you'd like, and there are cookies by the register; help yourself."

"No thank you," she said in a dismissive tone that sent a chill up my spine.

This woman really did think I'd murdered Cal Parker.

Which meant I had a lot more to worry about than whether or not I owned Seaside Cottage Books.

t was almost one in the morning by the time the investigators finally left. I spent a good half hour cleaning up the broken glass beneath the back door, as well as the fingerprint powder that dusted the floor beneath it. Then I shoved the papers into the desk drawer and slid it back into the desk; I was too tired to sort through them now.

One of the officers had helped me tack a board from the back shed over the broken window, but if, as Detective Ramirez claimed, the hole was too small for someone to reach through and unlock the door, somebody was either a skilled lock picker or had a key to the store. In which case, why smash the glass at all?

I'd left the key under the back mat for Bethany from time to time over the past few months, before I managed to get a copy made. Had someone taken it and had their own copy made?

I didn't know how someone had managed to get into the shop, but I did know that I was getting both locks rekeyed the next morning. It was unlikely that the intruder would return after the cops had been all over the place, and nobody had ever broken into my rooms above the shop, but sleep came only in short bursts that night; even Winston had a hard time settling down.

When the sun started peeking through the curtains, I gave up on sleep and put on slippers and a robe. I wasn't ready to face the day, but the day was facing me. I made an extra-large pot from the bag of French Roast coffee Denise had brought me. As the comforting scent of the brew filled my cozy kitchen, I leafed through the recipe book for another cookie recipe to tackle that afternoon (assuming sales would continue to be strong), settling on one for a delicious looking caramel turtle bar, and filling Winston's bowl with kibble and a few bits of grated cheddar cheese from the fridge.

By the time I opened at 10:00, the locksmith and glazier had promised to arrive early that afternoon, and the only sign of last night's drama was the wood tacked over the windows of the back door. It was a busy morning; I'd hoped to have a chance to do some more baking, but with the flurry of customers coming in out of curiosity and need for reading material, there wasn't enough time to nip up to the kitchen.

It was a rewarding morning, though. I introduced the grandmother of a young reader to the Boxcar Children, then helped her slake her interest in Ireland with Tony Hawks' *Round Ireland with a Fridge* and the first books of the wonderful Irish mystery series by Erin Hart and Sheila Connolly. We also ordered an Irish cookbook for her, as well as a book on Irish genealogy; she'd come back to pick them up in a week. I gave her two shortbread cookies as a bonus. I sent a visitor who had fallen in love with Maine on her family's vacation home with *The Secret Life of Lobsters*, the first of Lea Wait's Maine mysteries, and Bernd Heinrich's *A Year in the Maine Woods*, along with a gorgeous coffee table book on sea glass. By the time I'd sold my tenth book of the morning (*The Essex Serpent*, a creative magical historical book set in England), I was realizing I had a knack for finding the right book for the right person... just as Loretta had done for me.

As the woman with *The Essex Serpent* headed for the door, thanking me for my help, I recognized Agatha Satterthwaite marching up the front walk, looking (as my mother liked to say) loaded for bear.

"Good morning," I said as she pushed through the front door.

"You shouldn't be doing business," she said. "This place doesn't belong to you."

"I know you're contesting the ownership," I said, trying to sound reasonable, "and I'm looking into it, but if I don't sell books, I can't pay for the electricity or even groceries."

"You and Loretta stole from me," she complained. "You owe me hundreds of thousands of dollars."

"The whole thing is rather confusing," I admitted. "Why would Loretta claim to own the whole store if she didn't? And why didn't you take it up with Loretta?"

"What was I supposed to do, harass a dying woman?" she spat.

"But she passed a month ago," I said. "Why are you only bringing this up now?"

For the first time, she looked a little less sure of herself. Her eyes darted around for a moment, and then she said, "I had to research things."

"What things?" I asked. "If you knew the will gave the store to both of you, and you had a copy, what more was there?"

"I just... anyway, it doesn't matter when I lodge the complaint," she announced, crossing her arms over her chest. The buttoned-up collar of her gray blouse was so tight it looked like it might be cutting off circulation to her head. "We need this resolved. You need to pay me fair market value for my share of the property."

"If that is the answer, that's going to take some time, I'm afraid," I said. "I put all of my money into the store; I'd have to get a loan, and that's a process." I wasn't sure I could get a loan, but I wasn't going to tell Agatha that.

"You'll need to do it fast. I have a good offer on the property. If you can't match it, then I'll have to sell to him."

"But if I own half the property—and since Loretta signed a quitclaim deed, I do own at least half—then wouldn't I have to approve the sale, too?" I asked. "Besides, you'd have to pay my half of the value, since Loretta sold to me."

Her mouth worked for a bit; I'd flummoxed her. "All I know is you're a squatter. Maybe even a killer. And I demand my money." And then, without another word, she stormed back the way she'd come, leaving me feeling like I'd won at least a tiny victory.

For now, anyway.

But it still didn't get me any closer to getting me off the suspect list for Cal Parker's murder.

19

*B*ethany showed up at noon, looking pensive.

"What's up?" I asked.

"I've hit a bit of a stumbling block on my mystery," she said. "I know the timing is less than ideal, but would you mind if I announced the store mystery writer's group we'd talked about? I could use some input from fellow writers."

"I've got enough of a mystery myself to contend with right now, with half the town and the police convinced I killed Cal Parker," I said, "but go for it. Anything that brings people in the door is good in my book." It had been a slowish morning. I'd sold a few cookbooks, a couple of thrillers, and one copy of *The Very Hungry Little Caterpillar*, and eaten half the cookies myself.

"I'll put the notice on the Facebook page," she said, then hesitated. "There are a few things I should show you, by the way."

"What?"

She pulled up Facebook on her iPad. "You've gotten a few nasty posts from sham accounts."

"Like what?" I asked.

She scrolled to two of them. DO NOT SHOP HERE UNLESS YOU WANT YOUR HEAD BASHED IN, read one, along with BOOKSTORE OWNED BY MURDERER. The posters were named John Eastport and Jane Schoodic.

"Creative," I said with a sigh.

"I've hidden them all, but I had to change the settings on the page so that all posts are approved, and I have to monitor comments constantly."

"Who is doing this?"

"I don't know," she said, "but it's not good for business."

"Maybe we should shut down the page."

"Or, better yet, solve the mystery of what happened to Cal Parker," Bethany suggested. "Any ideas?"

As I rearranged the bookmarks I'd set up by the register —I hoped soon to have crafts from locals to sell, including handmade bookmarks and journals, presuming I remained in business for more than a week—I gave her a rundown of what I knew so far. "It had to be someone at the bookstore that night, since the murder weapon was the flatiron I keep by the door."

"Okay," she said, taking out a pad and a pen. "Meryl Ferguson is high on that list."

"Yes," I said. "She's furious he 'stole' her selectman seat, and thinks he was going to sell out Snug Harbor."

"But is that enough to kill for?" Bethany asked.

"I'm not sure it's typical 'crime of passion' material," I admitted, "but it's enough to keep her on the list. Jared Berland down at the Salty Dog is another possibility; Cal was giving him a really hard time about his business, and I overheard Jared and Sylvia yelling at each other down on the beach. She seemed to think he might have been respon-sible for what happened."

"Jared does have a violent temperament," she said,

tapping her pad with the pen. "I'll put him down. He's got a reputation for potential domestic abuse, too."

"Poor Sylvia," I said.

"I know," she said. "What about Cal's brother Josiah?" she asked.

"I've never met him, but from everything I've heard, he's definitely on the list," I replied as I moved over to the blank book section, straightening the spines. Would anyone ever buy them? I wondered, then banished the thought. "Do you know where I can find Josiah?" I asked.

"I'd recommend the Salty Dog," she suggested. "He likes to go there for Happy Hour and trash talk his brother with the Berlands."

"I can kill two birds with one stone, then," I said. "So to speak. On the other hand, Jared wasn't at the reading that night."

She chewed on the end of her pen. "When did you notice the doorstop missing?"

"Not until the end of the night, I think," I said. "Why?"

"I saw Jared and Josiah walking on the beach behind the store earlier in the day," she said. "They were talking intently. If the back door was unlocked..."

"Are you thinking one of them might have slipped in and stolen the doorstop without anyone seeing them?"

"It's entirely possible; I don't know if the back door was locked, so someone could have come in without our noticing" she said. "We don't know that it disappeared during the signing, after all. We can't rule anyone out."

I sighed. "This just gets more complicated, doesn't it?"

"It does. Speaking of complicated... what about romantic motives?" she asked. "Greed, revenge, and jealousy are three big motivations. We've got greed and revenge... but what about jealousy?"

"There's Jared, of course. He's got both jealousy and greed, not to mention possible revenge."

"That puts him in the top suspect position, I would say," she said.

"Cal's ex-wife Gretchen was at the store, too," I said. "Maybe she was jealous of his new girlfriend? Or thought he still had a little something for her in the will, and thought he was going to change it?"

"They've been divorced for a while," Bethany pointed out. "I would think that he would have changed his will right after the divorce... assuming he even needed to. He had a pretty ironclad pre-nup, from what I hear."

"You're probably right," I said, sinking down in one of the comfy chairs I'd scattered around the store for readers to enjoy. If only there were readers here to take advantage of them. And shoppers. Being a murder suspect did not appear to be good for business. Had I made a mistake by buying the store? Natalie had told me to follow my dreams... but what if I'd been wrong? "What a mess," I said, staring forlornly at the quiet cash register.

"It's just a setback," she said. "Look, I'll bet Josiah will be down at the Salty Dog for lunch today. Why don't you go down and see what you can find out from him, and I'll do some more poking into Kirsten online?"

"Are you sure?"

"Positive," she said. "Besides, this might help me shake loose my own mystery issue!"

~

THE SALTY DOG was bustling when I walked in. I hadn't been there in a few years, but not much had changed. Nautical maps and prints of sea creatures and old sailing ships adorned the raw wood walls, and varnished pine tables were filled with what appeared to be a healthy mix of locals and tourists. The smells of fried fish and beer perfumed the air as I let the door close behind me and headed toward the bar. Bethany had been right; I recognized Josiah from the Facebook profile picture she had shared with me, sitting at the end of the bar with a tankard, talking intently with the bartender, who I guessed was Jared. Josiah looked a lot like Cal, only in hippie form. Same chin, from what you could see under a good bit of bristly brown shrubbery. Same straight nose, same light eyes... only where Cal exuded success, you could read the bitterness on Josiah from across the room.

I walked over to the bar and sat down two stools away from him. "I think you should be good," Josiah was saying. "If they have another election, Meryl..."

Jared glanced over at me and stiffened. Josiah looked to see what his friend had reacted to; when he saw me, his eyebrows shot up.

"Hi," I said to Jared. "I'm sorry to interrupt."

"Weren't interrupting," Jared said in a surly tone, swiping at the bar with a rag. Like Josiah, he wore a thick beard, but had about forty pounds on his friend, and his arms were the size of tree trunks. He reminded me of a bear—and not a friendly one. If I were Sylvia Berland, I wouldn't want to cross him. In fact, even though I wasn't Sylvia Berland, I still didn't want to cross him. "What can I do for you?" he asked.

"Just a Pilsener and a basket of fried clams, please." I couldn't afford them, really, but I had to do something to justify my presence at the bar.

Besides... fried clams.

"Coming right up," he said, shooting a warning glance at Josiah before turning to grab a mug.

"Hi," I said, turning to Cal's brother and extending a hand. "I'm Max Sayers; I just bought the bookstore in town."

"Josiah Parker," he said, ignoring my extended hand. I caught a sour whiff of something stronger than beer as he spoke.

"Oh... I heard about your brother," I said, pulling my hand back. "I'm so sorry."

"Thanks," he said curtly, taking a swig of his beer and then turning to examine me more intently. "My brother was giving you a hard time about the store, wasn't he?"

I swallowed, my mouth suddenly dry. "Do you mean the permitting issues?"

"Oh, I'm not accusing you of killing him," he said. "Not totally, anyway," he added, giving me another speculative glance. "Cal gave everyone a hard time. Had to line the pockets, even though they were already full of gold. He always had to be the big man, throw his weight around."

"It doesn't sound like you miss him much," I said.

"I do and I don't," he said frankly. "Jared here certainly won't," he added, taking another sip of beer as Jared plunked a mug down in front of me.

"No, I won't," Jared admitted. "But that doesn't mean I had anything to do with what happened to him," he said in a warning tone to Josiah.

"Of course not, buddy. How could you? We were down at my place all night, finishing up that keg of Whale Tale Ale."

"Good thing we've got an alibi," Jared said. "Or they'd probably drag both of us down to jail." Jared cut me a look. "It was your doorstop that did him in, I hear."

"That's what I hear," I said. "Fortunately for me, half the town was in the store that day."

"It happened behind your shop," Jared pointed out.

"On public property," I retorted.

He shrugged.

"I hear Cal was giving you a hard time about your business, too," I said.

"He was," Jared admitted. "Trying to gouge me for my liquor license. He was messing with everyone in town. I think he was trying to turn Snug Harbor back to the way it was during its glory days. Tryin' to drive out the old stalwarts and bring in some higher-end stuff."

"It was like the Palm Springs of the Northeast back in the 20s, wasn't it?" I asked.

"It was," Jared said. "My grandfather used to get his booze from your house during prohibition," he said.

"I heard something about that," I said. "Even his wife didn't know."

"He had to hide the loot outside the house so she wouldn't find it, the story goes. Kept the details hidden somewhere; nobody ever found them."

20

"*Y*ou mean like a treasure map?"

"Or a journal... something like that. He used to walk over to Snug Island at night sometimes. Story goes it's hidden over there somewhere, but no one's ever found it."

"How did he keep all the booze hidden from his wife?"

"He did all his business while she was at church," he said. "And he walled off half the basement; it was all hidden behind shelves, with an outdoor entrance she didn't know about."

"How did he manage that?"

"He built it while she was in Boston. Everyone in town knew about it but her."

"Sounds like a marriage built on trust," I said dryly.

"She never wanted for anything," Jared said, glancing down the bar toward the door to the kitchen. Was Sylvia back there? I wondered.

"At any rate, everyone's always said he left something in the house to point to where he hid his ill-gotten gains, but after all these years, nobody's ever found anything."

"Loretta didn't tell me anything about that."

"Of course she wouldn't," Josiah said with a snort. "She's already looked for it, is my guess, and decided it must have been just idle speculation."

"Keep your eyes peeled, is all I'm saying," Jared said.

"And we'll be happy to take fifteen percent for tipping you off," Josiah said.

I laughed and said, "I'll keep that in mind." As I spoke, Sylvia emerged from the kitchen, looking wan and tense. "Fried clams?"

"Right here," I said, admiring the basket of golden fried deliciousness. "Those look amazing."

"Thanks," she said, a small smile of pride crossing her face. "A lot of people like 'em with tartar sauce, but I prefer them plain."

"Me too," I said. "Thank you."

"My pleasure," she said. She darted a look at Jared, who had tensed when she appeared, and vanished back into the kitchen.

"Don't ever get married," Jared advised Josiah when the swinging door closed behind her.

"Awww... Sylvia's one of the good ones," Josiah said.

"Need another?" Jared asked, pointing to Josiah's mug.

"Please," he said. "The same."

"Coming right up," Jared said, and poured him a fresh one.

"HOW'D IT GO?" Bethany asked when I got back to the bookstore a little while later.

"They both have an alibi," I said. "They were drinking together at Josiah's that night."

"Drat," she said, then cocked her head. "They could be lying."

"They could," I said. "I heard all about the history of the store, too... at least the Prohibition chapter of it."

"The whole hidden ill-gotten gains story? I'm not sure how much of that is true and how much is local legend," she said. "This house has been inhabited pretty much constantly since that time, and Loretta even renovated it into a bookstore, and nothing's been found."

"Do you think that's what my intruder might have been looking for? Some sort of map?"

"It's possible," she said. "The newspaper ran an article on Prohibition-era Snug Harbor not too long ago, and mentioned the role of Loretta's ancestor as the town liquor procurer. But I'm guessing it has more to do with some documentation that might show that Agatha sold her share to her sister."

"You think Agatha was the intruder?"

"It seems the most likely option."

"Hmm," I said. "I am curious about the cellar."

"Want to take a look?"

"I've been down there before, but it couldn't hurt."

"I'll make sure the bell on the front door is working and we can check it out together," she said. "It does feel creepy down there; I've only been down there a handful of times, but I don't like being there alone."

"If the stories are true, the only thing he stored down there was liquor."

She shivered. "I have a feeling there's more to the downstairs than rum and whiskey," she said. "Maybe it's this mystery I'm writing, though. I put an ad in the local paper; I'll be hosting the first meeting this weekend at the store, if that's okay."

"Sounds terrific!" I said as she opened the door to the cellar and turned back to me. "Ready?"

"Ready," I said, and together we descended into the basement.

It was a big, empty room, just as it always had been, with rock walls.

"It's big, isn't it?" she said. "You can tell where they dug it out to make it bigger than the house."

"It doesn't look big enough to store liquor though, does it?"

"Not for the whole town, no," she said. "You can see where people got in and out, though," she said, pointing to the hatch doors that led to the back yard.

We walked around the place for a bit.

"This is disappointing," she said. "Nothing here."

"No," I said, running my hand along one of the dusty walls. My finger slid into a groove between the rocks. "What's this?" I asked.

"I don't know," Bethany said. "It doesn't look mortared in."

"It's not," I said. I pulled at the edge; one corner of the stone moved. "There's something here," I said.

"Let me help!" Together, we pulled out the rock and laid it down on the stone floor. Bethany shone the light of her phone into the opening.

"It looks like some kind of old radio," she said as the light flashed on brass dials and a dusty wooden case.

"It is," I said. I could tell from the size of it that a few more rocks would have to come out to use it; sure enough, the ones beneath the one we had moved were also unmortared. "It's even got headphones."

"Why would someone hide a radio down here?" she asked.

"Rumrunners needed to communicate," I said. "I'll bet this is how he hid it from his wife."

"Wow," she breathed. "I wonder what else is here?"

"Let's find out," I said, and together we removed the rest of the loose stones. When we were done, she shone her light around the radio. There were a few cigarette butts in one corner, and something shiny. I picked it up and turned it over in the light from Bethany's flashlight. It was a Wheat Penny from 1913. "No one's opened this for a long time," she breathed.

"Nope. It's not treasure, but it's an indicator that not all the rumors are wrong."

"Let's put the rock back and look some more," she said. As she spoke, the bell rang upstairs.

"Coming!" I hollered, and together we heaved the rock back into place and headed up to the shop.

WE DIDN'T MAKE many sales, but we had a lot of what my mother used to call "lookie-loos" in and out. Bethany had to go home, so we abandoned further inspection of the cellar for now, but my interest was definitely piqued; I planned to do some research on rum running soon, to see what the radio was all about.

Things were slow for a bit, at least long enough for me to get the baking started. I'd just started measuring out flour when the bell at the door downstairs rang (I hung it on the doorknob when I had to go upstairs) and I heard Denise's voice ring out.

"I'm upstairs baking!" I called down. "Come keep me company!"

"I brought scones," she said. "We can eat them while we

wait for whatever you make to come out of the oven. What are you baking?"

"Chocolate toffee bars," I told her as she bounded up the stairs, bringing a buoyant, sunshiny energy with her. I smiled just seeing her; for a moment, it was as if all the decades, with their joys and heartbreaks, had never happened, and we were both twelve years old again. "Tell me more about those scones!"

"Cranberry walnut," she said. "With clotted cream on the side."

"No. Really? I haven't had that since I visited England and went to a tea room in the Cotswolds!"

"Good for the soul, if not the waistline," she said. "I brought coffee, too, of course."

"Of course," I said, smiling. "I made a big pot of French Roast this morning; it was amazing. I don't know if you heard about the excitement here last night, but it made it hard to sleep."

"No. What happened?"

As she pulled two plates from the shelves above the sink and laid out the scones, I told her what had happened.

"And the police think you somehow faked the break-in? Why?"

"I don't know," I said. "But there was no broken window when someone was in the store the other night, although I can't swear that the back door was locked."

"Maybe they got lucky the first time and had to break in the second time," Denise suggested.

"Maybe. But what were they looking for?"

She shrugged. "Hard to know, but maybe we should do some poking around for secret compartments ourselves."

"Bethany and I did that today," I said. "In the cellar. We

found an old radio hidden in a rock wall; I'm guessing the rum runners used it to communicate."

"Not exactly treasure, but that's really cool," she said. "Think that's what whoever it was was looking for?"

"I doubt it," I said. "But who knows?"

"I'm just glad they weren't in your cozy little apartment here," she said. "It does look good, by the way. That sea glass mobile in the window is gorgeous!"

"Thanks," I told her with a smile, looking at the mobile I'd made from a piece of driftwood we'd found on the beach when the girls were little, with strings of blue, green, and brown glass dangling down from it: blue at the top for sky, green in the middle for the water, and brown at the bottom for the sand. "I made it with my girls many years ago," I said, "from glass we picked up in on the shore in the summers."

"How are they doing with everything, by the way?" Denise asked as I combined the flour, brown sugar, and salt for the cookie base.

I sighed. "I think they're both okay," I said, "but Caroline is struggling with it more than Audrey. I get the impression she's not sure who to be angry at. I don't know if Ted is having the same experience I am—we haven't talked much the past few months, trying to get some separation—but I know it's been hard on her."

"And Audrey?"

"She seems relieved that the tension is gone," I said as I cut butter into the flour mixture and reached for the eggs. "Honestly, I wish I could say what went wrong. I still care for Ted, and he cares for me... we just hit a point where all the years of disconnection and frustration built up so much that neither of us could figure out a way to break down that wall. It's like once you have so many bricks, it's no longer possible to see over it to the other person."

"That's a great description," Denise said.

"All we can do is love the girls and support them and hope one day they'll understand," I said. "At least that's what I tell myself when I don't hear from Caroline for a month and a half." I added chocolate chips, then set aside some of the dough and patted the rest into the pan, then put it into the oven. Once it was done baking, I'd pour condensed milk over it, then sprinkle it with toffee chips, chocolate chips, and the rest of the dough and bake it for another half hour. The result would be a decadent bar cookie I had a hard time not devouring all at once.

As the crust baked, I sat down and broke off the end of a scone, slathering it with clotted cream before popping it into my mouth. "This is divine," I told her after I'd washed it down with a swig of hot coffee. "I have no idea how you manage to stay so thin."

"Good genes," she informed me as she bit into her cream-covered scone. "By the way, I saw your author friend today."

"She's not my friend. Was my ex with her?"

"No." She shook her head. "She just ordered a skinny latte. While she was there, she had a run-in with some woman at the coffee house. I don't know what they were talking about, but it seemed pretty intense."

"What woman?"

"She's pretty. Big glasses, dark hair. Drives a fancy green car. She ordered an espresso and said her name was Deirdre."

"Oh," I said. "That's Cal's girlfriend. I met her there yesterday. I wonder if she came back?"

"They didn't seem to get along well at all. The Deirdre woman was practically screaming at Kirsten, something about it all being her fault, although the espresso machine was so loud I couldn't make out what she was talking about. Kirsten finally just got up and walked out on her, but she looked pretty upset."

"Weird," I said.

"Yeah," she agreed. "I saw her talking with Cal Parker the night of the book signing; it looked a little tense, but I didn't think anything of it."

"I saw them too," I said, remembering seeing him stop to chat in the signing line, "but she was talking to everyone. What's their backstory, do you think?"

"Let's look it up," Denise suggested. She pulled out her phone and typed in their names.

"Aha," she said. "Look; they were in a society photo in Portland about four years ago."

"So they dated," I said.

"Looks like it," she said. "For at least a year; here they are the previous fall, at a charity gig in Bangor."

"She was there the night Cal died," I said. "She could have taken the flatiron before the signing." I tried to remember if I'd seen it after we opened the store, but I didn't remember.

Denise put down her scone and looked at me. "Are you suggesting that your ex-husband's girlfriend murdered Cal Parker on the beach behind your store?"

"She had means. She had opportunity."

"What about motive?" Denise asked. "Chuck you in jail so that Ted couldn't come back to you?"

"That ship sailed long ago," I said.

"She doesn't know that," Denise said. "But it's still a pretty weak motive for murder. I mean, most small busi-nesses don't make it anyway..." She opened her mouth wide and covered it with her hand. "Oh, my gosh. I can't believe I said that. I'm so sorry, Max... I just wasn't thinking!"

"It's okay," I said, even though it didn't feel okay. What had I been thinking, buying this place, not getting a title search, and putting all of my money into this store? And why did my heart still ache a little at the thought of Ted with another woman? "I know you were just thinking out loud," I said.

She leaned forward and put her hand on mine. "I promise I will do everything in my power to help you make things work."

"I just hope it will be enough," I said.

21

*O*nce Denise had left, I finished making the chocolate toffee cookies (eating six of them warm) and spent a good bit of time on my computer, compulsively looking up pictures of Kirsten Anderson. She was very glamorous, very successful, and had definitely been an item with Cal Parker. If they'd broken up, why did he come to her signing?

A bad thought came to me, then.

Did Ted know about him, and about Kirsten's glamorous past with the rich selectman?

And was it possible that he'd killed the man out of jealousy?

No, I told myself. My husband of almost two decades— and the father of my daughters—wouldn't be capable of such a thing. I felt traitorous for even thinking it.

I was scrolling through images of Kirsten looking annoyingly gorgeous when the front door opened, and Ted himself walked into the shop.

I jumped, almost falling off my chair. Then I quickly closed the window on my screen—a head shot of Kirsten in a low-cut black V-neck blouse—and looked up, forcing a smile. "What brings you here?" I asked. He was so familiar, and yet there was a distance between us that was unfamiliar.

"We're staying at the Ivy Gate Inn. Kirsten's writing, so I decided to come check on you. I heard that you had a bit of a nasty surprise."

"You mean finding the dead selectman next to the shop?" I asked.

"Yeah. That," he said. "Are you okay?"

The concern in his eyes made my heart hurt a little. "I am," I said. "But that's only part of the problem."

"What do you mean?"

I told him about the title issues.

"I wish you'd told me what you were doing," he said. "I've got contacts; I could have helped you."

"I know you would have, but I wanted to do it myself," I said.

He nodded. "I understand."

We were quiet for a long moment, and then I asked, "Do you know if K. T.—Kirsten—knew Cal at all?"

"She hasn't mentioned it," he said, his eyebrows going up a bit. "Why do you ask?"

"Oh, you might want to talk to her about that," I said, shrugging. "So. How was the lobster dinner after the signing?"

"We didn't go. Kirsten had a bit of a headache, so we went back to the hotel and heated up some chowder. She knocked off early, so I went and grabbed a few beers at the Salty Dog." He cocked an eyebrow. "Wait a moment. Are you suggesting one of us might have had something to do with what happened to that selectman?"

I debated what to do. I didn't want to interfere in his life, but there had been a murder. After a moment's hesitation, I decided that Ted probably should know what I knew. "Someone mentioned that she and Cal used to go to things together," I said. "Charity dinners and stuff."

He shook his head. "She never mentioned it."

"I understood they exchanged a few words the other night."

"Kirsten and Cal?" He looked startled, and then gave me a suspicious look. "Are you suggesting that the woman I'm dating is a murderer?"

"No!" I said. "I just... I'm trying to figure out what happened. I was hoping maybe if she knew him, she could shed some light on the situation."

"Why does it matter?"

I held up my stained fingertips. "Because I don't want to go to jail," I said.

And even though chances were slim, I also didn't want my children's father sleeping in the same bed as a murderer, I thought but didn't add.

THE REST of the afternoon was slow, but I was anxious, feeling like I should be doing something, but not sure what it was. Once the store closed, I took Winston for a quick walk, then went upstairs and put on moose PJs and my favorite slippers, even though it was only eight o'clock. I made myself a sandwich, giving Winston a little bit of my turkey, then pulled my cookie recipe book out of the shelves and flipped through until I found one of the girls' favorites: oatmeal thins.

I called Audrey as I gathered the ingredients, but my call went straight to voicemail. I called Caroline next; same thing. Sighing, I put down the phone and focused on the cookie recipe—and the issues that had haunted me since the book signing.

I had just pulled the pan out of the oven when the phone rang. I glanced at it; it was Ted. Twice in one day! I felt my shoulders tighten, and my heart rate sped up. "Hello?" I said cautiously when I picked it up.

"Someone's... someone's attacked Kirsten," he said.

"What? What happened?"

"I don't know," he said. "I just got back from picking up Chinese food, and she's... there's blood everywhere, and she's unconscious, and I don't know what to do, and..."

"Oh my God," I said. "Where are you?"

"At the Ivy Gate Inn," he said. "Room 232."

"Have you called 911?"

"Yes; they're coming."

I wasn't surprised he'd called me; I'd been in charge of all medical issues from the time we got married, and he'd been happy to leave it all to me. It must have been automatic to call me when there was a medical crisis. "All right, hang in there. I'm on my way."

22

*T*he Ivy Gate Inn was one of Snug Harbor's beautiful former cottages, and only a few blocks from the bookstore. I parked my CRV on the street and hurtled into the reception area, where a startled-looking young woman stood behind the front desk. I glanced down at myself and could see why; I was still in my moose pajamas, with giant bear-paw slippers on my feet. "Where's Room 232?" I asked.

"Up the stairs to the left," the woman answered, then said, "Can I help you with something?" but I was already thundering up the stairs.

I pounded on the door, and Ted swung it open. He gave me a quick up and down. "Wow."

"I was in a hurry," I said tartly. "Where is she?"

"Over here," he said, pointing to the enormous king-sized bed. There, sprawled across the satin coverlet, was Kirsten, wearing a silk teddy. Her oval face was pale, and her dark hair was matted with blood.

"Oh, no," I breathed. "That's a bad head wound. Is she breathing?"

"She is," he said, running a hand through his thinning hair and kneeling by her side. The tenderness in his eyes as he brushed a stray hair from Kirsten's face felt like someone pressing on a bruise.

"Who could have done this?" I asked.

"I don't know," he said. "I went out to pick up food, and when I came back..."

I knelt beside her and reached over to take her pulse. Her skin was clammy, but warm. "Her heartbeat is strong, at least. And her breathing's steady, so that's positive; I don't think there's anything we can do until the paramedics get here but monitor her, unfortunately." I scanned the area. "What was it that hit her?"

"A rock. It's over there." He pointed to the corner, where a bloody rock lay. Blood mottled the wallpaper; it looked like whoever had hit her had hurled it at the wall in anger.

I sat back on my heels and took in the room. A plastic bag with two styrofoam containers lay on the floor by the door; from the scent of ginger and garlic, I was guessing it contained Ted's favorite Chinese takeout dish, Kung Pao chicken. "Did anyone see you leave?" I asked.

"Just the front desk person, I guess," he said. "I wasn't really paying attention. She called in the order about forty-five minutes ago, and put it under my name. I left a half hour ago; I was only gone about twenty minutes."

"Was the door ajar when you got back? Did you lock it when you left?"

"What is this, the third degree?" he asked, a familiar touch of asperity in his voice.

"I just want to understand what happened," I said. "Cal Parker was hit over the head, too. I'm wondering if the same person attacked both of them."

He looked up at me, and our eyes met over Kirsten's prone form. "I don't know what I'll do if she dies."

Again, the pain welled in my heart. I was glad we were no longer married—we hadn't been a good match—but seeing him care for another the way I'd wanted to be cared for was hard. "I'm sure she'll be fine," I said with a calmness and confidence I did not feel. "Do you know of anyone who might have wanted to harm her?"

"Of course not!" he said. "Everyone liked her."

"Did she talk with anyone while she was in town?" I asked. "Anyone she knew?"

"Only her fans at the store," he said. "We've spent most of the time... well... here," he said, flushing as his eyes strayed to her silky teddy. When Ted and I had walked down the aisle just over 20 years ago, this was about the last situation I pictured us being in a few decades down the line.

"She was dating Cal Parker once," I reminded him.

"But he's dead!" he said.

"Yes," I said. "But it's possible that whoever attacked him also attacked Kirsten. Maybe it was somebody they both knew."

"No," he said, shaking his head vehemently, and again running his hand over the top of his head, a familiar gesture. "This has got to be random. A break-in gone wrong. A burglary..."

"Is anything missing?" I asked, putting a finger on Kirsten's wrist to monitor her pulse, which was disturbingly fluttery; would the EMTs ever get here? We both glanced around the room; the drawers were untouched, and there was no sign of anything being rifled through.

"Not that I can tell," he said.

My eye was caught by a button on the floor. "What's this?" I asked.

"I don't know," he shrugged, squinting at it. "Maybe it was from the previous guest and the maid staff missed it. Who cares? I just want her to live."

I grabbed my phone and took a picture of the button; there was a bit of light blue fabric still attached to it, as if it had been ripped off a shirt cuff or collar. Had Kirsten done that trying to defend herself? I glanced down at her hand; one of her manicured nails was broken, and a bruise was blooming on her left forearm. A defensive wound?

Almost automatically, I glanced at my ex-husband's shirt; to my relief, he was wearing a collared polo shirt, which I didn't recognize but was yellow and had all of its buttons attached. I pulled up my phone camera again and took a picture of the rock in the corner. Would Kirsten survive? I wondered. Would she be able to tell us what happened?

And was I right that the same person had attacked both Cal and Kirsten?

And if so... why?

~

IT FELT like hours before the paramedics arrived.

"Is she going to be okay?" Ted asked as they squatted over her.

"We'll take her in and do everything we can," the taller of the two said.

"She'll be okay, though?"

"We'll let the hospital staff evaluate her," the woman said tersely, glancing up at her partner. "Our job is to stabilize her and take her in; you'll have to talk with them. Are you family?"

"She's my girlfriend; we're together," he said.

"Does she have family?"

"Her mother," he said. "She's in Portland... should I call her?"

"Better safe than sorry," she replied, which told me all I needed to know. The outlook wasn't good.

I didn't recognize the police officer on duty who came shortly after the paramedics, but he recognized me. As they worked on Kirsten, he turned to me. He looked just a few years older than my daughters. So young.

"You're the one who found Cal Parker, right?" he asked, tablet in hand. He had freckles and red hair, and looked like one of the boys in a Norman Rockwell painting. Except for the technology and the police uniform, that was.

"Right," I said.

He glanced over to where the paramedics were strapping Kirsten to a stretcher. "How do you know the victim?"

"She's my ex-husband's girlfriend," I said.

"Ex-husband's girlfriend," he repeated slowly. "And how did you come to be in their hotel room?" he glanced around. "This is their hotel room, right?"

"He called me when he found her. I usually take... er, took care of medical issues in the house. I came over to be with him."

"So she was already down when you got here?"

"That's right," I said.

He glanced over at my ex-husband, then asked, in a low voice, "Is your ex-husband a violent man?"

"He never laid a finger on me the twenty years we were married," I told him. "This happened while he went out to pick up Chinese food."

"She was attacked while he was gone," he said, not sounding convinced. "Is that what he told you?"

"It is," I said. "But Kirsten Anderson and Cal Parker used

to date. I think whoever killed him may have attacked her, too."

He glanced over at Ted again. "Used to? Is your ex the jealous type?"

"I told you, he didn't do it," I said. "Look; I found a button on the floor; it looks like it was torn off of a blue shirt. My husband... er, ex-husband's wearing a yellow shirt."

"He could have changed before you got here," the young officer pointed out. I guessed that was true. "You referred to him as your husband," the officer then pointed out unhelpfully. "Where were you this evening, Miss..."

"Sayers," I told him. "Max Sayers. I was at the bookstore until Ted called."

"Was anyone with you?"

"My dog," I said.

"I won't ask him to give you an alibi," he said, his mouth twitching into a slight grin. "Can anyone else confirm your whereabouts?"

"Not after I went up to my place, above the shop. We closed at six; I think the last customer was at 5:30."

"Who was that?"

"It was a tourist; I'm sure I can look up the credit card information when we get back."

"Please do that," he said. He glanced over at the rock in the corner. "Recognize that?"

"It's a chunk of granite," I said. "Those things are kind of everywhere, aren't they?"

"They are," he admitted. "Going to be hard to trace that. Although maybe there will be fingerprints."

"Maybe," I said, not sure of how well rocks took fingerprints. "I just hope she's okay."

23

*I*t felt like weeks had passed by the time I left the Ivy Gate Inn, still thinking on what had happened as I closed the front gate behind me and looked back up at the imposing building. Although Ted and Kirsten had gone to the hospital, the lights in their corner room were still lit, and I wondered what had happened in Room 232. Had Kirsten sent Ted to pick up dinner so she could meet someone in the inn, and had it gone wrong? I couldn't imagine meeting a lover for a ten minute rendezvous while your boyfriend went out to pick up Chinese, though; nor could I imagine greeting anyone I wasn't interested in romantically wearing a silk teddy. It didn't make sense. I got in the car and drove down the darkened street away from the inn, passing Scooter Dempsey's office as I turned the corner. The office windows were darkened, but the dim streetlight faintly illuminated the horse in the painting over the reception chairs. Scooter and Cal had been business partners of sorts; would he have any inside information on the connection between the attacks on Cal and Kirsten?

My nerves were on edge the whole way back to the shop;

even though it was only a few blocks, it seemed like miles. I locked the door behind me and double checked the rest of them, grateful that there was no sign of broken glass or forced entry.

I headed upstairs and got ready for bed, brewing myself a cup of chamomile tea and snuggling into bed with Winston, but even the latest Tonya Kappes camper mystery couldn't calm my racing mind. The little Bichon was unperturbed, and curled up calmly beside me, but I found myself anxious, half-listening for the sound of breaking glass downstairs. I'd had a second lock installed on the door to the apartment from the shop, and I planned to get a security system soon, but the budget only went so far, and after what had happened tonight, I was more than a bit on edge.

I put Tonya's book aside a few chapters in, then tossed and turned for an hour, the image of Kirsten's blood-matted hair appearing every time I closed my eyes. Sleep wasn't coming; I needed something to take my mind off things. And one of the benefits of living right above a bookstore is that you have 24-hour access to a smorgasbord of literary distractions.

Winston half-opened one eye as I wrapped myself in a bathrobe and unlocked the door to the stairs, hitting the light switch as I made my way down to the shop below.

My eyes darted to the glamorous head shot of K. T. Anderson standing on the table of her signed books. Was she doing okay? I'd texted Ted, but hadn't heard back. I considered the stack of *Fast Money* books on the table. I hadn't read Kirsten's latest, and wasn't sure I wanted to. I debated it for a moment, then morbid curiosity won out. As I reached for one of the signed hardbacks on the stack, I realized I still hadn't done anything with the copy behind the counter from the signing; the one Scooter had asked Kirsten to sign, then abandoned at the cash register.

Sure enough, the copy of *Fast Money* was still there, tucked in with the Dick Francis book Scooter had brought to the register. I reshelved the Francis book in the signed books/first editions section, then headed back upstairs with KT Anderson's latest in my hand.

I grabbed a cookie and took it to bed with me, trying not to get crumbs on the percale sheets as I took a bite and cracked open the thick book.

I turned first to the title page, on which Kirsten had written a dedication in a controlled, neat hand.

To Scooter, she'd written. *Without you, this story never would have been written. Thanks for inspiring me. — KT*

Inspiring her? I didn't know Kirsten and Scooter had ever met, much less that he had been a muse for one of her bestselling books. I turned the page and started Chapter One. Kirsten's protagonist was a scrappy young investigator named Megan Garcia, and the case in question involved some untimely deaths at a horse-racing track in New Hampshire. No wonder Scooter had picked up the book, I thought to myself; the topic certainly was up his alley. Had he told her about the world of horse racing? Had that been what inspired Kirsten's story?

I spent the next few hours devouring the book; Kirsten was a fluid stylist, and the pace was relentless. The story focused on a horse-racing scandal in a small town in upstate New York. Someone was hiding something... and people and horses were dying, in the most gruesome way. It wasn't until the last few chapters that I understood what the dedication meant. My blood ran cold as I read the last chapter.

Then I grabbed my phone and googled a name. It popped up immediately, in a flurry of news articles that dated a year before Kirsten's book was released... no doubt when she was writing. I searched the community pages for pictures of Kirsten and Cal. The last one appeared a month after the news stories hit. Had they broken up? If so, why?

I had a theory. If Kirsten came to, I could confirm it with her... but barring that, there was one place I might find what I was looking for.

The problem was, I had to get in and out unseen.

I HARDLY SLEPT AT ALL; I spent the night searching the internet, rereading sections of Kirsten's book, and piecing together what I suspected. Bethany arrived at 8:30 the next morning, right on time, thankfully.

"You look exhausted. What's wrong?"

"Someone attacked Kirsten last night," I said.

"Oh, no!" Bethany's hand leapt to her mouth. "Is she okay?"

"Ted and I have been texting; she's stable, but she hasn't come to. I hope she wakes up soon. I think the solution to Cal Parker's murder is in this book, but I want to talk to her and make sure I'm on the right track." I held up a copy of *Fast Money*.

"Wait, what? A fictional mystery solving a real-life mystery?"

"Yes," I said. "I can confirm it with her when she wakes up... but I'd like to find out sooner than that, so that no one else gets hurt."

"What's your plan?"

I told her.

"I don't like it," she said.

"I'll take my phone and I'll be in and out," I said. "If I find something, I'll tell the police."

"Why don't you tell the police first?"

"I just need to find one thing first," I told her.

NINE O'CLOCK FOUND me sitting across the street from Dempsey Development, a tumbler of coffee in my hand and adrenaline coursing through me. The doors were closed and locked until Rupert sauntered up at 9:12, coffee cup and keys in hand, and let himself in. He turned on the lights, flipped open his computer, and busied himself at his desk for a few minutes before picking up the phone and launching into a long, apparently very engaging conversation. I hoped he'd finish soon, or have enough coffee that he needed a trip to the facilities. Preferably before Scooter Dempsey turned up.

Finally, at 9:38, Rupert stood up and headed down the hallway. He opened a door in the hallway, turned on the light, and stepped inside, shutting the door behind him.

I sprinted across the street and eased the door open, then trot-tiptoed down the hall, past the closed door, to Dempsey's office, praying the door wouldn't be closed and locked.

It wasn't. I slipped inside, closing the door behind me most of the way. As I hurried over to the desk, I heard the sound of a toilet flushing; a moment later, the door in the hallway squeaked open, and footsteps headed back to the front, away from Dempsey's office.

I scanned the desk first; there was an untidy pile of open mail on the corner, in an overflowing wooden tray. I flipped through it; there were several past-due bills, as well as a letter from an investor that caught my interest:

. . .

DEAR MR. DEMPSEY:

IT HAS BEEN some time since you proposed the Cottage Street project in Snug Harbor. Although we are interested in investing in the project, the delay in beginning the project is proving to be a major concern. Unless the properties in question required for the development have been acquired and the permit process begun by the end of July of this year, we will have to divert the funding to a different project.

KIND REGARDS,
    Phoebe Floyd
    Vice President
    Coastline Recreational Investments

WELL, that was good news for me; if I held out till August, the threat of development would apparently no longer be an issue. I took a quick picture of the letter and moved on.

There were several bills from contractors for projects in Bangor and Kennebunkport; they were all marked ninety days or more past-due. Scattered through the stack were a number of little scraps of paper that looked like receipts. They were receipts of a kind, I realized. Blazoned across the top was SCARBROUGH DOWNS TRACK. Each slip of paper was a bet... some for fifty dollars, some for three hundred, one for as much as two-thousand dollars. There were several bets per day; I found five, totaling $5,000, for the previous weekend. Had any of them won? I wondered.

I looked at the stack of unpaid bills. Was Scooter gambling away all the money he was supposed to use to pay contractors? I snapped a few pictures of the racing stubs and looked back at the letter from the development company. Glancing at the door and wondering how much time I had left, I pulled up Google and typed in the name of the development company.

Although the board of directors included no one I recognized, the owner was yet another company, named Windswept Holdings. And guess who owned Windswept Holdings?

Cal Parker.

I glanced at the letter from Coastline Recreational Development. It was dated five days ago: two days before Cal Parker died.

It was as I suspected.

In Kirsten's book, a developer with a penchant for horse-racing used projects to piggy-back off each other, growing bigger and bigger debts, but paying off each one with proceeds from the newer one. I'd thought that Cal Parker had been involved, too; in the book, the investor and developer were working hand-in-hand to make things go, with the investor getting onto the local board to help with permits for the project. But now I wasn't so sure Parker had anything to do with Dempsey's Ponzi scheme. Either that, or he read the book and figured out what was going on, then pulled the financing.

I was guessing that someone had tipped Cal Parker off as to what was going on with his developer friend—Scooter was fairly recognizable—and that was why he pulled the funding. If Parker wouldn't move the project forward, Dempsey's house of cards would all fall down. And if it was Kirsten Anderson's book that tipped Parker off to Dempsey's problems, then Dempsey would certainly have a bone to pick with the author. His office was right down the street from her hotel. He would have seen Ted leaving... and been able to head up and do the deed before he came back with dinner.

I sat back in Dempsey's leather chair, piecing everything together. Dempsey must have been desperate for the money from the development project to pay off the contractors on his other projects... and feed his gambling habit. The text message made sense now; Dempsey had contacted Parker to see if he could sweet-talk him into changing his mind.

With the book dedicated to Scooter and a picture of the letter from Coastline Recreational Development—not to mention the racing stubs—I hoped I had enough to convince the police to at least get a search warrant.

But first I had to get out of Dempsey's office.

I peeked out the door into the hallway, looking for a back door. I didn't want to walk through the front office, announcing my presence to Rupert, if I could help it. I tiptoed across the hall and peeked into the conference room. No door. I was about to head up the hall and brazenly walk out the front door when a familiar voice drifted down the hall.

It was Agatha Satterthwaite.

"I'm here for my ten o'clock with Mr. Dempsey," she said.

"He'll be here any minute, I'm sure," Rupert said. "You can wait in one of the chairs."

She didn't respond, but I assumed she took him up on his offer. I debated what to do; should I walk out the front door blithely? Or wait to see if I could find out what she and Dempsey had cooked up to get me out of my shop?

The question was almost immediately rendered moot.

I heard the outer door of the office open.

"Good morning, Mr. Dempsey," came Rupert's syrupy greeting.

"Good morning, Rupert," Scooter replied, followed by, "Agatha! So good to see you. I'll be with you in just a moment." I ducked into the conference room as he marched down the hall to his office. Had I left everything in order? I fretted. Would he know someone had been in his office?

It didn't matter now, I reflected. I would wait until they were cozied away in his office, and then I would walk out the front door and go straight to the police.

But that wasn't how it worked out, of course.

*a*s I tried to stay calm and wait for my opportunity, footsteps sounded in the hallway. "Are you ready, Agatha? Let's get started. Come on down to the conference room."

The conference room?

I whirled around, looking for a place to hide. There was a shelf with construction trophies on it (at least that was what I guessed they were; they had buildings on them) and a closet with a small set of folding doors at the far end of the room. I scurried over to the closet and yanked the doors open. The closet was filled with file cabinets. The only place to hide was on top of them.

As their voices approached, I hoisted myself up onto the nearest cabinet, squatted, and spun around to close the doors behind me. I got them almost closed when Agatha walked in; holding my breath, I released the doors and tried to melt back into the shadows.

"Glad to see you," he said, closing the conference room door behind him. "I've been meaning to talk to you; have you had any luck getting your hands on that copy of the contract?" As he spoke, I turned my phone to camera and hit "record." It couldn't hurt, after all.

"No," she said. "I looked, but I can't find it anywhere. I don't know where she could have put it!"

"We need to find it if we're going to go forward," he said. "The last thing we need is litigation down the line."

"I know," she said. "What if I can't find it? Will you still buy it from me?"

"Yes... but at a reduced price," he said.

"How reduced?"

"At least fifty percent," he said. "The cost of litigation would be huge. If someone finds that contract stating that you sold your share to Loretta, then there could be consequences; you'd owe Sayers the money you got from the sale, and she could sue both of us for damages. "

"Do you think she'd really do that?"

"I would," he said.

"But if you tear down the house, all the evidence would be gone."

"It's still a risk that it could turn up. Did you look in the basement?"

"No," she said. "Why would she hide something in the basement?"

"You know that house used to be a rum runner's stash. I'm sure there's a good hiding place down there; if I were going to keep documents, I'd see what I could find down there."

"I'll look tonight," she said.

"I heard you almost got caught," he commented.

"I did," she said. "But I'll be more careful this time. You'll still buy it even if I don't find the contract?"

"I will," he said. "As long as we can convince Sayers that it's time to sell."

"I know how to do it," Agatha said in a tone of voice that sent chills up my spine. "It will solve both of our problems; you have to promise me not to discount the original sales price, though."

"What's the plan?"

"Burn it," she said flatly. "Burn the whole thing down. Those books will go up like kindling, and all our problems will be gone."

"Burn Max, too?"

"Oh, no. I'd wait till she was gone; if she dies, then there's probate, and there are more people to talk into selling the property. If the store's gone, she'll have no choice but to sell. Even if insurance pays out, it will be at least a year before the store can be rebuilt and restocked. She'll lose the whole summer's revenue, and possibly next year's, too."

"I like it," he said slowly. "I think that'll work, actually. We need to get this done soon, though, or the deal will fall through."

"I'll do it tomorrow morning," she said. "She usually takes her dog for a walk. Once they leave, I'll toss a gas-soaked rag through the window and then a match."

"That should do it," he said. "Although the arson might hold things up. Is there a way we can do it without the gasoline?"

"I'll see what I can do," she said. "Shall we touch base tomorrow afternoon?'

"Sounds good," he said. As they stood up from their chairs, my phone rang in my hand.

"What's that?" Agatha said sharply as I stabbed the red button to reject the call.

"There's someone in the closet," he said.

"They heard everything!" Agatha gasped.

"I'll take care of it," Scooter said in a tone of voice that made my blood run cold. He yanked the door open. Agatha let out a little scream, but Scooter just narrowed his eyes.

"Change of plan," he said, turning to Agatha. And then, smoothly, he grabbed one of the trophies lined up on the shelf and brought it down on my head.

~

WHEN I CAME to with a splitting headache, I was still in the closet, only bound hand and foot. Still on top of the filing cabinet, though. I turned and pushed my feet at the closet doors, but they didn't budge; someone must have secured them from the outside.

I kicked at the door, but nothing happened.

"I wouldn't bother if I were you," came a familiar voice. It was Scooter's, of course. "I gave Rupert the rest of the day off after Agatha left. We're just waiting for it to get dark."

"Bethany will want to know where I am."

"No worries. We texted her from your phone. She knows you're out of pocket today. You told her to close up early and go home, and told her you'd pay her extra for taking over. Once it gets dark, we'll take you home."

"And then what?" I asked.

"You'll find out," he said.

A scream built up in me; I could only imagine what would happen. They'd burn the store with me in it, make it look like an accident. "Please let Winston go, at least."

"I'll think about it. In the meantime, please shut up. I have things to do today. First, though, I need you to sign something."

"No," I said automatically.

"If you sign it, I promise to let your dog go free. We'll write you up a nice suicide note, saying you couldn't face the failure of the business and your marriage together. We'll make sure your dog is nowhere near the building when it happens."

"You want me to sign a contract selling the shop to you, don't you?"

"You always were smart," he said. "It's too bad things had to end this way... but it's better if we can make sure at least one thing you love survives, don't you think?"

He opened the closet and handed me the contract.

"I can't read it with my hands tied behind my back," I said.

"Yes you can," he said. "I'll hold it for you."

I glanced at the words on the front page as he held it up for me. It was a contract to sell the property, for cash, to Dempsey Developers, effective immediately. "You killed Cal, didn't you?" I asked. "Because he was going to back out on you."

"He was a fair-weather friend," he admitted. "I thought I could talk him into an extension, but after our conversation, he decided to withdraw the offer immediately. Your ex-husband's girlfriend caused me a lot of trouble."

"How did she find out about you?" I asked.

"Cal and I used to like to go to the track together," he said. "We'd both wager. For Cal, it was fun, but for me, it's... well, it's my lifeblood. Kirsten figured it out, did a little poking around, and asked me a lot of questions about the racing... how the odds worked, etc. I told her everything I knew. Then I found out she was talking to some of my contractors... she poked into my private business. She and Cal broke up a while back. It wasn't until I met Cal on that beach and he confronted me about the gambling, about what was in Kirsten's book, that I realized how much of my situation she'd used."

"And that's why you killed him?"

"No. You know how Meryl Ferguson's been on him ever since she lost that election to him? Like a dog with a bone. She was chatting up Cal's dingbat girlfriend the other day, and Deirdre was stupid enough to tell Meryl that Cal was investing in some big project on the waterfront in town, and that she had an inside scoop. Cal was furious at her for saying anything—she threatened to tell Meryl he was the main investor in the project if he didn't agree to marry her. It didn't work, of course, but he told me he had to cut the project loose; it was too risky."

"Cut it loose? Or just give you a shorter timeframe?"

"He was going to tell the board to kill it completely. So I had to kill him. He was going to ruin me." He shook his head. "I never should have left that stupid book in the store. If I'd known what she meant, I never would have left it behind." He ran his hand over his head, his movements jerky. "I just wasn't thinking straight; I'd just gotten that letter, and I was mad." He looked up at me. "I came back later to get the book, but I couldn't find it."

"So you broke into the shop?"

"Once," he said. "And Agatha did on her own, too, as I'm guessing you've figured out."

"I gathered from the conversation," I said. "So, how far in debt are you?"

"A couple hundred grand," he said. "When this deal comes through, I'll be able to pay that off and still pocket a good chunk of change."

"When? I thought Cal's company put a time limit on it?"

"How do you know that?" He was quiet. "Oh, I see. You were in my office, too. How did you manage that?"

"I waited until Rupert had to use the facilities," I admitted. "I watched from across the street. Just like you watched for Ted to leave the hotel before you confronted Kirsten."

"That's right," he said. "She ruined my life. I had to make her pay. She used me for her book, made all that money off of me, and then ruined me. If she hadn't written that book, none of this would have happened." He grimaced. "And I'm still not sure if the job's done."

"She's still alive?"

"Word is she's still in a coma at the hospital. I'll have to visit her this afternoon. In fact, thank you for reminding me. I'll go now. We can do this later."

"But..."

"I'll be back," he said. He took off his tie and wrapped it twice around my face, over my mouth, to make a makeshift gag. "I never did like this tie, anyway. Don't go anywhere," he added, then chuckled at his own bad joke. As I recoiled at the taste of his dirty tie in my mouth, he left the conference room and hurried down the hallway.

I had to warn Ted.

But how?

25

I quickly took stock of my situation. My hands were bound behind my back and my feet were tied together. My phone was long gone. And with a gag in my mouth, I couldn't talk even if I could figure out how to find a phone and somehow manage to dial it.

I had only one option that I could see.

Channel my inner gymnast.

I didn't have much time; the hospital was only a few blocks away, and it would only take a minute or two with a pillow to end Kirsten's writing career prematurely.

I took a deep breath and tried to relax my body, then swung my legs over the edge of the filing cabinet. The cabinet was too tall for my feet to reach the floor, so I shimmied over to the edge and then dropped, almost losing my balance and falling face first; I hopped wildly, lurching forward, until my shoulder hit the wall. Slowly, with little hops, I got myself into a standing position, then hopped over to the conference room door, praying he hadn't locked it.

He had, of course.

I turned around and hopped over to the window facing the alley beside the office and pressed myself up against the glass, searching for a passerby who would make eye contact. Unfortunately, nobody was in the alley. A cat wandered by and gave me a slitty-eyed look, then sat down and began to clean its back legs. I groaned. How was I going to get someone to see me?

I started shoving my shoulder at the glass, hoping I could break it. I'd hop back a few steps and then hurl myself at it. The glass thumped, but nothing else happened. On the third try, I managed to fall over; I had to inch back to the window and get my feet underneath me, then slide back up so that I was standing.

Time was running short; it had already been ten minutes. Was Scooter already at Kirsten's bedside with a pillow in his hand?

I couldn't wait any longer.

I backed up further, and with all my strength, hurled myself at the glass window.

This time, I didn't bounce back.

The glass shattered as I hit it and I hurtled to the pavement, landing hard on my shoulder. I yelped with pain from behind the gag.

There were footsteps, and a young couple stood over me, both holding coffee cups from Sea Beans; they must have been walking by the mouth of the alley when I fell through the window

"Are you okay, Miss?"

I made a few squeaking sounds, eyes bulging.

"She can't talk with the gag on, Mike," the young woman said. She handed her coffee to her friend, squatted down and unwrapped the tie from around my head. "Who did this to you?" she asked.

"Do you have a phone?" I gasped.

"Of course," she said, as if I'd asked her if she had lungs. "It's right here. Let me untie you first."

"First call this number for me and put it on speaker, okay?"

"What? Why? You're bleeding! We need to get you to a hospital!"

I looked down to where a small puddle of blood was gathering on the pavement under my arm; I'd gashed it on the broken glass. My hip wasn't feeling terrific, either... nor was my head. "Please. I'll explain in a minute; there's no time." As I dictated Ted's number, she dialed it in. I prayed that Ted would pick it up; after the third ring, he did.

"Ted, it's Max. Scooter Dempsey is on the way to the hospital; he killed Cal Parker and now he's going to try to finish off Kirsten."

"What? How do you know this?"

"It doesn't matter. Are you at the hospital?"

"Yeah. I'm in the cafeteria."

"Go upstairs. Now. And call the police."

"I'm going," he said.

"Call me back," I said. "Okay if he uses this number?" I asked the young woman, who was staring saucer-eyed at the phone.

"Sure," she said. "Maybe we should call the police, too? This is just... What's going on?"

"Wait until he calls back," I asked.

"This is crazy. I can't believe this is happening in Snug Harbor. Who is Ted, anyway?" the young man asked, fumbling with the knots at my ankles as his girlfriend freed my hands

"My ex-husband."

"And who's Kirsten?" the young woman asked.

"My ex-husband's girlfriend." The two exchanged looks. "It's a long story," I said. "I'll explain it once he calls back."

"Right," the young woman said. "I'm Sasha, by the way, and this is Mike."

"Max Sayers," I said.

"Great to meet you," she said. "What can we do to help you while we wait for your ex-husband to call back?"

"Maybe help me get the glass out of my arm?"

"Let me get this knot undone first," Mike said, still struggling with the bonds at my feet."

"I'll help," Sasha offered.

"Thanks," I told them.

As the two worked on the knot, a few people drifted up.

"Is this some kind of movie set or something? What happened here?" asked an older man with a Pomeranian.

"Kidnapping," I said. "And murder."

"Murder? That woman you called about?"

"Among other things." I didn't mention my own breaking and entering. Was it breaking and entering if you walked into an unlocked office? I wondered.

"Does this have something to do with the selectman they found on the beach?" the man asked.

"Yes," I said. "Would someone mind calling the police? We're waiting for a call on Sasha's phone."

"Oh. Duh. Of course," Mike said, pulling his own phone out of his back pocket and dialing 911.

"Yeah," he said when someone answered. "We're outside of this office called..."

"Dempsey Development," I supplied.

"Dempsey Development. Some lady named Max just fell out of a glass door; she was all tied up, and apparently someone's trying to kill her ex-husband's girlfriend." Silence. "No, this isn't a joke," he said. "I'm serious. Get someone over here please; and maybe an ambulance, too. She's hurt." Silence again, and then he said, "Thanks. I know it sounds weird, but it's just that kind of day. Yeah. Thanks. We'll just wait here then, right?" He hung up a moment later, just as Sasha's phone rang.

She picked it up and put it on speaker phone. "Ted?" she asked.

"It's me," he said, his voice ragged. "You were right. He was in here with her, trying... trying to kill Kirsten."

"What did you do?"

"I hit him," he said. "Knocked him out. The cops are on their way, but... but Kirsten's okay. Thank you," he said, his voice ragged. "How did you know?"

"He told me," I said, suddenly feeling weak. "I'll explain it all later." As I spoke, there was the sound of a siren. I let my head drop to the sidewalk and closed my eyes just as the paramedics hurried over to me. Kirsten was safe. Scooter Dempsey was soon going to be in custody.

And now I knew Agatha had signed the bookstore over to her sister.

It had been one heck of a morning.

EVEN THOUGH MY wounds were superficial, the EMTs insisted I go to the emergency room anyway. The police, of course, had lots of questions about how I had ended up in the middle of an alley in a pile of glass, bound hand and foot with inside information on an upcoming murder. I promised to fill them in on everything once I got the rest of the glass out of my forearm, stopped bleeding everywhere, and had access to Ibuprofen.

I was in the emergency room getting bandaged up and

preparing for an X-ray to make sure I hadn't broken anything on the way down to the pavement when Ted burst into my little cubicle.

"Are you family?" asked the nurse who was dressing my wounds.

"I'm her ex-husband," he said. "The police told me you were here... are you okay?"

"You're not supposed to be in here," the nurse said. "Only family."

"He's family," I said, again feeling that twist in my heart. We might be divorced, but we had raised two children together. Not everything ended just because a marriage did.

"Are you okay?" he asked again, and there was genuine concern on his face.

"I am," I said.

"What happened?"

"I overheard Scooter and Agatha talking about their plans for the bookstore. Scooter found me... then he tied me up and then went to kill Kirsten," I said. "He was planning to burn the bookshop down later, probably with me in it."

"What? Why? Didn't you know him as a kid?"

"I did. It's a long story. Is Kirsten okay?"

"She is," he said. "Thank you so much for calling. If you hadn't..." He shivered. "He was there when I got there, with the pillow over her face. If I'd been a minute or two later, it would have been too late."

Thank goodness for Mike and Sasha, I thought.

"She came to earlier, by the way," he said. "They think she'll make a full recovery."

"Thank goodness. Did they arrest him?"

"They did," Ted said, sitting down on one of the plastic chairs. The nurse, while quietly attending to my wounds, had perked up her ears. "How did you know he killed Cal Parker and attacked Kirsten?"

"I read her book," I said. "It was all in there. She used Scooter as a model for one of her characters."

"She knew he was a murderer?"

"I don't think she knew he'd stoop to that—she took liberties—but she figured out he had a gambling habit and was playing fast and loose with the numbers at his business to make things work. Cal read her book and figured it out pretty fast. I'm guessing he did a little poking around into Dempsey Development's current projects. In any case, he threatened to back out of the development deal with Scooter. Scooter was counting on that money to keep everything afloat... when he couldn't talk Cal around, he killed him and tried to pin it on me."

"You'd be an obvious suspect for Kirsten's attack, too," Ted said. "Although I know you'd never do something like that."

"I wouldn't," I concurred as the nurse continued to bind my wounds. Very slowly, I noticed.

"All good," she said reluctantly. "The tech will be by soon to take you to X-ray." She smiled at me. "I hope your life gets less complicated soon."

"Me too," I said. "Thanks."

When she left, Ted took a deep breath and looked at me. For a moment, we were just as we were years ago, before all the distance and misunderstandings and resentments grew into a mountain neither of us could scale. "I miss you sometimes," he said. "I care for Kirsten, but you and I've got a lot of history."

"I know," I said. "I miss you sometimes, too."

"Can we be friends?" he asked.

I thought about it for a moment. "Maybe in a little while," I said. "I think we both need to heal some first."

"Yeah," he said, looking away. "Even though it was probably the right thing, it's still hard. Audrey is doing okay, but Caroline is still struggling, I think."

"Did she say anything to you about it?"

"She told me she doesn't like Kirsten," he said. "I don't know what to do."

"I don't know either," I said. "But they'll have to work it out, won't they?"

"I guess," he said. "I've been meaning to ask... is the store going okay? Sales good?"

"Better than expected so far," I said. "Fingers crossed. Kirsten's signing was a big boost. I'm grateful to her for coming."

"She's a good person," he said. "I think you'd like her."

"We'll play it by ear," I told him, not quite ready to become BFFs with Ted—er... Theodore's new flame. "Anyway, thanks for coming by."

"Do you need a ride home?"

"I'll call a friend. Thanks, though."

He stood up, putting his hands on his lower back and stretching, a movement I'd seen thousands of times before. "I'll go back up to keep Kirsten company, then. Thanks for saving her."

"You're welcome," I said. "They're supposed to send officers in to talk to me, but I think with all the excitement over Kirsten, they may have forgotten where to find me. Can you send them down and ask if I can have my phone back?"

"I'll track someone down," he said. "Let me know about the hip, okay? And send any medical bills to me."

"Right," I said. "Thanks."

And he walked out of the emergency room, leaving me feeling more alone than I had in a long time.

Until thirty seconds later, when Denise rushed into the room, Bethany at her side.

"Ohmygosh," Denise said, coming up and giving me a careful hug that filled my heart with love and warmth. Bethany followed suit as Denise said, "I heard Scooter hog-tied you and threw you in the middle of the street, then went to strangle your ex's girlfriend! And he's the one who killed Cal Parker?"

I laughed. "I'm still waiting to talk to the police, but you got most of the story, if not the details. I threw myself into the street, not Scooter. And where did you hear all this?"

"We saw the cops going down the street, and some guy with a Pomeranian told us about a woman crashing through the window and talking about a murder, so we pieced it together from that. The police haven't been in to talk to you yet?" She looked at my bandaged arm. "Is that going to be okay?"

"I think so," I said, and gave her my version of events.

"So real life followed the story in Kirsten's book," Bethany said, eyes wide, as I finished telling the tale. "That is so cool! If she hadn't written that book..."

"Cal Parker might still be alive," Denise said. "They always say the pen is mightier than the sword, but I never took it literally. That's so sad!"

"Kirsten didn't make it happen," I said. "She simply wrote what she saw. Scooter was the one who got himself into trouble and killed to try to get out of it."

"True," Bethany said. "And Kirsten almost paid with her life. She's going to be okay, isn't she? I'd hate it if she stopped writing!"

"Looks like she'll be fine," I said. "Thanks for coming. I

know we're supposed to keep regular store hours, but I'm glad you're here.".

"Are you kidding?" Denise asked. "With everything that happened, you're going to get tons of publicity... half the town is going to come in just to see if they can find anything out!"

I laughed. "From your lips to God's ears," I said as the tech came in to take me to X-ray.

THE NEXT MORNING dawned clear and chilly. After making myself a double latte and drinking it with a maple walnut scone from Sea Beans, I whipped up a batch of chocolate chocolate chip cookies (they were like round brownies with walnuts). As the last batch cooled on racks next to the oven, I leashed up Winston and hobbled down to the beach behind the shop—my bruised hip reminding me of its existence with every step—hoping that I'd find a few good bits of sea glass during the low tide.

It was a beautiful morning. Gulls wheeled overhead, bright white against the blue sky, and the breeze off the water was salty and fresh.

Not long after Denise and Bethany had come to see me, the police had finally showed up to take a statement from me. They'd even returned my cell phone after taking prints and downloading a recording of the conversation between Scooter and Agatha. I didn't have a piece of paper documenting the sale of the property to Loretta—yet—but I at least had a verbal confession that Agatha had signed the shop over to her sister before I bought it. Plus, the police had assured me they'd be charging Agatha with accessory to attempted murder, or something like that, and potentially fraud as well. I didn't know what all that meant for the shop's future, but with Scooter in jail and Agatha most likely on her way, I was hoping not to have to worry about that for a bit.

I had enough on my plate as it was.

As I walked, the phone rang. I glanced down; it was Caroline.

"Hi, sweetie."

"I just got off the phone with Dad," she said. "Is it true you saved Kirsten's life?"

"It is," I said.

"And somebody tied you up and was going to burn you and the shop up? I thought Boston was scary, but I'm worried about where you're living now!"

"It was a one-time deal," I said. "I'm fine."

She was quiet for a moment.

"It's good to hear from you," I said quietly.

"I've... I've missed you," she said.

"I've missed you too," I told her gently.

"Can I maybe come up and see the shop?" she asked. "I can stay with grandma if it's easier; I know you don't have a lot of room."

"I'd love for you to stay with me—there's always room for you—but stay wherever you feel most comfortable. I'd be delighted to see you and show you around."

"All right." She paused. "This weekend, maybe?"

"That would be wonderful, sweetheart," I said.

"Shoot... I've got another call, but I'll plan to drive up Friday. I'll let you know what I decide about where to stay. Okay?"

"Got it," I said. "I'll even make your favorite cookie bars."

"The ones with toffee and chocolate chips?"

"The ones with toffee and chocolate chips."

"You're the best, Mom. Love you."

"I love you too," she said, and hung up. My heart swelled with love and relief.

As I put my phone in my pocket and refocused on the glistening rocks on the ground at my feet, Winston tugged at the leash. I looked up; a familiar form was walking toward me.

Nicholas.

"Hey," I said as he walked closer. He was so handsome... even more so than when we were kids. My heart pounded, and all of a sudden I felt like I was thirteen all over again, about to try to talk to my crush.

"I heard you had an exciting day yesterday," he said. "You okay?"

"Just a few bumps and bruises," I said, feeling self-conscious about my less-than-manicured state.

"Looks like more than bumps and bruises," he said, pointing to my bandaged arm. "That looks nasty."

"A few stitches, but it'll be fine," I said. "And at least I don't have to worry about the shop."

"Why not?"

I gave him the CliffsNotes version of what had happened yesterday.

"Sheesh. So Agatha was working with Scooter to try to defraud you," he said. "Scooter Dempsey always was a jerk. I just didn't know how low he'd stoop."

"You didn't know that twenty-five years ago?" I asked, arching an eyebrow.

"I did," he said. "But... I'm sorry I believed what he said about you. I should have been a better judge of character; I knew Scooter wasn't always honest, but it just... well, I was wrong."

"Thanks," I said as Winston sniffed at his khaki pants. He

bent and scratched the fluffy little dog's head, and Winston leaned into him. "Water under the bridge, right?"

"Maybe, but I still want to apologize. Can I take you to dinner to make it up to you? At least partially?" The sun glinted in his hair as he looked up at me, and my heart flip-flopped in my chest. "You still like fried clams?"

"I love them," I said.

"If you're free tomorrow night, I'll take you to Chart House. And I know you've got a confession recorded, but we should look for that document."

"You're right. Bethany and I found an old radio in the cellar the other day," I said, "hidden behind a rock. And a penny dating from before 1920."

"Aha! More evidence of rum runners."

"That's what I thought. Originally, I wondered if the folks breaking in might be after a treasure map or something, but it turned out it was just Agatha and Scooter."

"Still. Maybe there's a stash down there after all," he said. "Loretta's grandfather had to do something with all his ill-gotten gains; he sure didn't spend it on a mansion." He glanced at his watch. "If you've got some time before the store opens, I'd love to see that radio. There are a lot of stories about that place, you know."

"Sure! I just made cookies; you want one?"

"Of course," he said. Together, we turned and headed back to Seaside Cottage Books, Winston prancing happily ahead of us, glancing over his shoulder from time to time to check on us. The scent of the beach roses drifted through the air, and the sight of the little store with its sparkling windows—plus the presence of my teenage crush just a few feet beside me—made me feel like breaking into song. Which, thankfully, I didn't.

It was turning out to be a perfect day. Thank goodness

everything had settled down at the store, I thought as we walked next to each other down the beach.

But trouble was already brewing again... and was about to hit home a second time.

Closer than I liked.

FIND out what happens next in the second Snug Harbor mystery, *Inked Out,* coming soon. Reserve your copy for a chance to name a character in Max's next adventure! Get the details at Karen's web site... and while you're there, be sure to join Karen's Readers' Circle and download your free book!

RECIPES

MAX'S FAVORITE COCONUT COOKIES

Ingredients:

1 cup shredded coconut
1 cup self-rising flour
1 cup sugar
1 egg
1/2 cup melted butter

Instructions:

Preheat oven to 350F. Mix the dry ingredients together. Stir in the egg and then the butter with a wooden spoon, then work the dough together with your fingers.

Form walnut-sized balls with your hands (do not add more flour; they will feel greasy). Arrange on an ungreased baking pan, about two inches apart, and bake for 10 minutes. (Bake for a minute or two less for chewier cookies!)

BROWN SUGAR SHORTBREAD COOKIES

Ingredients:

3/4 cup butter
3/4 cup soft or light brown sugar
2 cups plain flour
pinch of salt
Additional brown sugar to coat rolls

Instructions:

Preheat oven to 350F.

Cream butter and sugar together with an electric mixer. In a separate bowl, whisk salt into flour, then add flour mixture to creamed butter and sugar and mix into a firm dough.

With your hands, knead the dough together and then form into two rolls, about 1 ½ inches in diameter.

Sprinkle brown sugar on wax paper, and roll the dough up

in the paper, coating the roll with the sugar. Chill wrapped dough rolls in the refrigerator for at least 30 minutes, preferably longer (the dough should be firm).

Unwrap the dough rolls one at a time (keeping each roll in the fridge until you are ready to bake it) and slice each roll into 3/16-inch disks. Arrange the disks on an ungreased cookie sheet and bake until the brown sugar around the edges colors, between 15-25 minutes, depending on how chilled the dough is.

RASPBERRY MELTAWAYS

Ingredients:

Cookies

1/2 cup unsalted butter, softened
1/3 cup confectioner's sugar, sifted
1/2 teaspoon vanilla extract
1 cup flour
2 tablespoons custard powder*
Confectioner's sugar, for dusting

*If you can't find custard powder, substitute 2 tablespoons of cornstarch mixed with 2 teaspoons of vanilla extract and a pinch of fine salt. Alternately, you can use instant vanilla pudding mix.

Raspberry Filling

1/4 cup unsalted butter, softened

1/4 teaspoon vanilla extract
3/4 cup confectioner's sugar, sifted
6 frozen raspberries, thawed

Instructions:

Cookies

Preheat oven to 325F and line 2 cookie sheets with parchment paper.

With an electric mixer, cream butter, sugar and vanilla until light and fluffy.

Sift flour and custard powder over creamed butter and sugar, and stir by hand with a wooden spoon until ingredients are just combined and a soft dough forms.

Form 30 balls, using 1 heaping teaspoon of dough per ball, and place on baking sheet, with room between balls to allow cookies to spread. Using a fork dipped in flour, lightly flatten each ball until dough is 1/3 inch thick. Bake for 15 to 20 minutes or until cookies are light golden. Cool on pan for 10 minutes, then transfer to a wire rack to cool completely.

Raspberry Filling

While cookies are cooling, make the raspberry filling. Using an electric mixer or whisk, beat softened butter in a bowl until light and creamy. Beat or whisk in vanilla. Add confectioner's sugar, and whisk until well combined, then stir in raspberries.

Assembly

Spread the flat side of one cooled cookie with one teaspoon of filling, then sandwich with a second cookie. Repeat with remaining cookies and filling, and serve dusted with confectioner's sugar.

CHOCOLATE TOFFEE BARS

Ingredients:

2 1/3 cups all-purpose flour
¼ teaspoon salt
2/3 cup light brown sugar
¾ cup butter
2 eggs, slightly beaten
2 cups semi-sweet chocolate chips, divided
1 14-ounce can sweetened condensed milk
8-ounce package toffee bits, divided

Instructions:

Preheat oven to 350 degrees F. Prepare a 9x13" baking pan by greasing it or lining it with parchment paper. Combine flour, salt and brown sugar in a large bowl, then cut in the butter with a pastry blender or fork until the mixture is crumbly. Add the eggs and stir to incorporate, then mix in 1 1/2 cups of chocolate chips.

Set aside 1 1/2 cups of the dough, and press the remaining dough into the 9x13" baking pan. Bake for 10 minutes.

Remove pan from oven and pour the sweetened condensed milk over the warm baked crust, gently spreading it into an even layer. Reserve 1/3 cup of the toffee bits; sprinkle the remaining toffee bits evenly over the condensed milk layer. Dollop the remaining dough over the toffee bits, and sprinkle with remaining chocolate chips and toffee bits.

Bake for 25-30 more minutes, or till golden brown, and cool completely before cutting into bars and serving (if you can wait that long). Store bars covered, preferably in the fridge.

MORE BOOKS BY KAREN MACINERNEY

To download a free book and receive members-only outtakes, giveaways, short stories, recipes, and updates, join Karen's Reader's Circle at <u>www. karenmacinerney.com</u>! You can also join her Facebook community; she often hosts giveaways and loves getting to know her readers there.

And don't forget to follow her on BookBub to get newsflashes on new releases!

The Snug Harbor Mysteries
A Killer Ending
Inked Out (Winter 2020/2021)

The Gray Whale Inn Mysteries
Murder on the Rocks
Dead and Berried
Murder Most Maine
Berried to the Hilt
Brush With Death
Death Runs Adrift

Whale of a Crime
Claws for Alarm
Scone Cold Dead
Anchored Inn
Gray Whale Inn Mystery #11 (2021)
Cookbook: The Gray Whale Inn Kitchen
Four Seasons of Mystery (A Gray Whale Inn Collection)
Blueberry Blues (A Gray Whale Inn Short Story)
Pumpkin Pied (A Gray Whale Inn Short Story)
Iced Inn (A Gray Whale Inn Short Story)
Lupine Lies (A Gray Whale Inn Short Story)

The Dewberry Farm Mysteries

Killer Jam
Fatal Frost
Deadly Brew
Mistletoe Murder
Dyeing Season
Wicked Harvest
Sweet Revenge (Summer 2020)
Cookbook: Lucy's Farmhouse Kitchen

The Margie Peterson Mysteries

Mother's Day Out
Mother Knows Best
Mother's Little Helper

Wolves and the City

Howling at the Moon
On the Prowl
Leader of the Pack

ACKNOWLEDGMENTS

First, many thanks to my family, not just for putting up with me, but for continuing to come up with creative ways to kill people. (You should see the looks we get in restaurants.)

Special thanks to my mother, Carol Swartz, for her constant encouragement and careful reading of the manuscript, as well as putting together character and book bibles to keep me straight! Thanks too to Abby MacInerney for proof-reading and general feedback. What would I do without you??? And a special thank you to Kate Pedersen for providing recipes, including Max's favorite coconut cookies. :)

Thank you SO MUCH to my Beta Reader Crew for your fabulous suggestions and corrections: Kay Pucciarelli, Brenda Crow, Gail Holzer, Tina Thomas, Melissa Clark Stephens, Kate Pedersen, Tarri Feden, Gina Waffles, Tanya Jackson, Julia Hunter, Martha Ellis, William Seward, Karen Clarida, Tyna Derhay, Katharine Horn, Mary McKenzie Keller, Federica De Dominicis, Patricia DeVito, Vicki Hardman, Karen Eberle, Kathleen Chrisman, Samantha Mann, Elizabeth Bonneau, Tricia Lento, Lisa Miller-Adkins, Kim Templeton, and Mary Sigler. You help me make Snug Harbor shine!

Thanks (as always) to Bob Dombrowski for his incredible artwork. Kim Killion, as always, did an amazing job putting together the cover design, and Angelika Offenwanger's sharp editorial eye helped keep me from embarrassing myself (as did Connie Leap's proofreading). And a special shout-out to Hollis Duty for helping me with covers, overall direction, and much, much more.

And finally, thank you to ALL of the wonderful readers who make Snug Harbor, the Gray Whale Inn, and Dewberry Farm possible, especially my fabulous Facebook community. You keep me going!

ABOUT THE AUTHOR

Karen MacInerney is the *USA Today* bestselling author of multiple mystery series, and her victims number well into the double digits. She lives in quaint Georgetown, Texas with her sassy family, Tristan, Little Bit, and a new arrival, an antique Chihuahua rescue named Jelly Bean (a.k.a. Dog #1, Dog #2, and Dog #3).

Feel free to visit Karen's web site at www. karenmacinerney.com, where you can download a free book and sign up for her Readers' Circle to receive subscriber-only short stories, deleted scenes, recipes and other bonus material. You can also find her on Facebook (she spends an inordinate amount of time there), where Karen loves getting to know her readers, answering questions, and offering quirky, behind-the-scenes looks at the writing process (and life in general).

P. S. Don't forget to follow Karen on BookBub to get news-flashes on new releases!

www.karenmacinerney.com
karen@karenmacinerney.com

facebook.com/AuthorKarenMacInerney
twitter.com/KarenMacInerney